LEVON'S WAR

A VIGILANTE JUSTICE THRILLER
BOOK 6

CHUCK DIXON

ROUGH
EDGES
PRESS

Levon's War
Paperback Edition
Copyright © 2022 (As Revised) Chuck Dixon

Rough Edges Press
An Imprint of Wolfpack Publishing
701 S. Howard Ave. 106-324
Tampa, Florida 33609

roughedgespress.com

Paperback ISBN 978-1-68549-041-6
eBook ISBN 978-1-68549-031-7

Special thanks to Alan Gordon and John Quinn of The Suffolk Sportsman for the loan of the Kalashnikov.

And a burst of automatic fire into the air for Steve Lowenthal.

LEVON'S WAR

1

Gunny Leffertz said:

"A man only has two things he truly owns. His soul and his word. And he can't keep one if he loses the other."

They heard gunfire in the night.

That was nothing new. The sound of guns in the desert was as common as the call for prayer.

Over the next day and night, the gunfire grew more frequent. The thunder of explosions drew closer.

Rona wanted to go to school. Kani wanted to play outside.

Their mother told them that there was no school; it was not safe to play outside. They shuttered the house and sat in darkness. The radio their only link to the outside. They heard no mention of their town.

And then there was no radio. Trucks moved on the streets outside. Then the helicopters boomed by to circle overhead. The gunships made long loops in the sky. The wind from their blades buffeted the house, making the shutters bang in their frames. There was a whooshing sound, over and over, from above. The rumble of distant explosions.

Pejma prayed for her daughters. She prayed for the return of her husband. She kneeled and prayed to Melek Taus, the angel of God, to deliver them from evil.

The helicopters went away. The gunfire died to silence. For the rest of the night and into the following morning, there were no sounds from outside.

"Mother, I am hungry," Kani said. She was the youngest, with all the selfishness of an eight-year-old child. All that she knew was that her belly was empty.

"I will go down to the market," Pejma said.

"No," Rona said. She was four years older than her sister, with an understanding of the world beyond her years.

"It will be fine. I will buy some bread and cheese and be right back," Pejma said. She freed her arm from her daughter's grip.

"Then take us with you," Rona said.

"It will be faster if I go alone," Pejma said.

She left her daughters and unlocked the door to step into the brilliant white light of the desert sun. She opened the gate to enter the street. It was a winding lane lined with houses concealed behind curtain walls. The houses were all shuttered just as hers was. No cars moved. The streets and walks were empty. A ribbon of black smoke moved across the sky somewhere down near the river.

She looked back at her own house. It was the finest home she had ever lived in, paid for by her husband's job at the refinery. A room for the girls alone and a bathroom with running water. Her husband was gone now to Mosul with the militia. She wished that he was here. She missed him with a physical longing. If he were here, she would not be afraid.

Pejma walked on toward the oil company store, the closest market to their home. Over the rooftops, she could see the stacks of the refinery. Something new fluttered from the tallest stack.

A black flag sewn with white letters in Arabic.

The men of the new caliphate were here, in Baiji.

But the soldiers promised them. The president promised them. The oil executives promised them. Baiji was too remote. Too small for the invaders to be interested in.

She wanted to believe that, that their size and location would keep her family safe and away from the fighting. She knew, in the end, that the oil would bring them here.

Voices came from around the turn in the lane ahead. Voices followed by the hum of a truck motor.

Pejma dropped behind the trunk of a palm and watched the men come around the curve and into view. Men in black weighed heavy with ammunition and carrying rifles. The truck that followed had a large black gun mounted in its bed. A smaller version of the black flag that flew from the refinery swung on a pole over the cab of the truck.

In front of the armed men trotted a man Pejma knew. Mr. Fakhoury, the man who ran the company store. She often saw him on her weekly trips to the market. Smiling and friendly and a few times allowing the girls to take free sodas from the cooler. He always asked after her husband. She would tell him of the most recent letters from Bazît, fighting somewhere with the YBS. Now the shopkeeper was leading the black-clothed men down the street toward her home.

Mr. Fakhoury was pointing at houses along their path. Each time he pointed, a group of the men would break off to kick their way into that home's courtyard. She recognized the homes as belonging to either fellow Yazidis, Shi'ite families or foreign oil workers.

Pejma was up on her feet, moving fast along a wall back toward her family's house.

She was not fast enough. Mr. Fakhoury called out to her, called her by name.

2

"Anthony Marcoon. United States Treasury. Interviewing Dr. Jordan Roth. The time is two-fifteen p.m. on October twenty-fourth."

"Is this about my wife?" Dr. Jordan Roth said.

The tall agent's eyes glittered for an instant. He coaxed a cigarette from a pack taken from his jacket pocket.

"Part of it. Mostly I want to talk to you about your son-in-law. Levon Cade."

"Could you please not smoke?" Dr. Roth said.

"You're kidding, right?"

"This is a no-smoking facility, isn't it?" Dr. Roth said. He nodded toward the sign by the door of the interrogation room. It confirmed the rule.

Prick, Marcoon thought. He hoped Roth could read that in his eyes.

"You'd rather be back in your cell, huffing bean farts? You can stand a little secondhand smoke." Marcoon fired up the Marlboro.

"What's your interest in my son-in-law? My daughter has been dead for years."

"You still have ties. Your granddaughter."

"I lost that fight when I had to go into hiding."

"And why was that, Doctor? Because you murdered your wife?"

Dr. Roth began to speak but decided against whatever he was about to say.

"Relax, Doctor. I'm not interested in who killed who. Huntsville homicide can clear all that up. I'm sure the Bureau will step in to help get you out from under those charges. And you can stop pretending to be a Cuban GP."

"In exchange for what?"

"I need some blanks filled in. Levon Cade's record is spotty. Lots of redactions. Some of it is *all* redactions. Help me get a better picture of the man."

"Is he in trouble?"

"If there's trouble he's *not* in, I haven't heard of it."

Dr. Roth smiled.

"What do you want to know?"

Tony Marcoon blew a stream of smoke to the ceiling before smearing the cigarette out on the tabletop.

"See? That wasn't so hard," he said.

———

"We've been looking in the wrong place," Marcoon said.

"For Cade?" Nancy Valdez's voice came from the speakers of the rental car.

"The only damned detail in his file we thought was right, is wrong. Cade's an Alabama boy." Marcoon sat at a light, waiting to make the turn into Miami International. Cars in front of him gleamed like beetles under the afternoon sun. He lowered the window to allow a blast of heat in through the crack. He tipped ash off his cigarette against the top of the glass.

"He was born in North Carolina."

"Born, sure. His mother had him at a hospital in Raleigh. She was staying with cousins living there at the time. Cade's father was not the most reliable guy in the world."

"And Cade told this to his father-in-law?"

"No. His daughter told him. Cade's not much of a talker, according to Roth. The Gary Cooper type."

"Who's Gary Cooper?" Nancy said.

"Ha ha. Old man joke. Fuck you too, Valdez," Marcoon said, and swung the wheel through the light onto airport property.

"So where do we look?"

"Roth says Cade was a pure hillbilly. Raised in a bumfuck town somewhere in the northeast corner of Alabama."

"He couldn't do better than that?"

"That's all he could remember."

"That's it? Not much."

"Oh, and his granddaughter loves Wendy's. Not much to go on."

"What did you promise him, Tony?"

"I told him we'd put in a word in exchange for his cooperation. You know. Blah blah."

"You've been down there for two days. Just grabbing some sun by the pool?"

"Naw. Took longer than I wanted. He was going to lawyer up. Wanted me to sign something, rope in a federal judge."

"Nothing like that's crossed my desk."

"He gave all that shit up for a solo cell." Marcoon pulled into one of the queues at Budget Rental and honked the horn for an attendant.

"Good man. Not much to go on, but better than what we had. Hurry back," Nancy said. She broke the connection.

A chubby attendant, face shiny with sweat, took the rental papers from Marcoon. He glanced from the Marlboro in Marcoon's fingers to the sign on the dash thanking renters for not smoking.

3

"Will it hurt?" Merry said.

"It's just a cleaning," Levon said.

"Why do I need my teeth cleaned? I brush and floss and all that."

"Because the dentist can get things you can't get. And take x-rays and like that."

Merry settled back into her chair to work on the Sudoku book she brought along. A habit she picked up from her Uncle Fern. Two moms were talking together in the waiting room while their kids, younger than Merry, played with a wooden train set. CNN was on with the volume down on a big flatscreen mounted on a wall decorated with cartoon bears and clowns.

"Mr. Cartwright?" the receptionist at the counter called. A pretty girl with short cropped blonde hair and glasses with big cat's-eye lenses.

"Yes?" Levon stepped to the counter.

"You didn't fill in any insurance information," the receptionist said. She held up the clipboard of forms he'd filled out with lie after lie.

"We don't have dental," he said.

"How will you be paying? Check or charge?"

"Cash."

"I hope we have change here." The eyes behind the cat's-eye lenses blinked.

"Moira?" a dental hygienist in a colorful smock said. She pronounced it 'MY-rah.' An attractive Asian girl. Levon wondered if the dentist was married. She stood in the waiting room, eyeing Merry with a professional smile.

"It's MOY-rah," Merry said. She rose and unhappily followed the hygienist toward the cubicles at the rear of the practice.

Levon retook his seat and idly watched the TV. A commercial for the best pillow you'll ever own ended, and the newscast returned. The host and two others argued at length over some minute change in the rules of order in the Senate. The discussion grew heated until the host ended it to turn to a breaking news story.

With greater interest, Levon watched a report from Iraq about an ISIS assault in the region of Mount Sinjar. A correspondent spoke over B-roll footage of black-clad terrorists firing a variety of weapons at unseen targets, interspersed with what was supposed to be a terrorist training camp where unfit men dressed like ninjas swung along monkey bars.

"The targets here, the victims, are the Yazidis, a local Christian sect that has called Sinjar home for millennia. The choice for these locals is clear. Convert to Islam, pay the tax that ISIS demands or face execution. Tens of thousands have fled into the heights around Mount Sinjar, adding to what is already a humanitarian crisis that demands the world's attention."

The reporter, speaking from a location hundreds of miles from the events of the story, fielded a few questions from the anchor before the segment ended. The anchor shared his deep concern for the people forced to flee before turning to a teaser about a celebrity putting her mansion up for sale, which led to a commercial featuring a young couple complaining about their car insurance.

Levon's eyes stayed on the TV, but he saw something far beyond the images there. He became aware of someone standing by him. The pretty hygienist with Merry by her side.

"Moira did very well." This time she pronounced it correctly. "No cavities."

"Told you," Merry said. She flashed gleaming whites.

"She could spend a little more time flossing her back molars. Plaque," the hygienist said.

Merry squinched her face.

———

They ate at Wendy's in Haley before driving home.

Merry told him a joke the dentist had told her. Levon only half heard her.

"Isn't that funny?" she said after the punchline.

"Sure was, honey."

"You didn't laugh."

"I'm laughing on the inside."

"I guess it wasn't *that* funny," she said. She mopped up some ketchup with the end of a fry.

"Sorry, honey. I don't know where my mind is."

"I'll bet you do."

"Do what?"

"I'll bet you know where your mind is," she said. Her eyes were on his.

"Just thinking about something a long while back," he said.

They finished up in silence before clearing their table and returning to the truck. They didn't talk much on the ride back to Uncle Fern's. Merry knew her father's mood and thought it best to let him be. She worked her last unfinished Sudoku in her head as the trees flashed by either side of the two-lane.

4

"Lone Star Solutions. Garrett here."

"Hey, Tobey."

"Shit."

"That any way to say hello?"

"I told you I helped you all I could, Levon. You are *radioactive*, man. Do you know the kind of time I could get just talking to you?"

"Remember Bazit Hassan?"

"Buzz-it? You know all those names start to run together. I must've known a hundred Hassans."

"This guy's a Yazidi. Helped us in the oil fields that time. You called him 'Pancho.'"

"Yeah. Yeah. Mean-looking fucker. Looked like a pirate crossed with a Mexican bandit."

"I need to know where he is. If he's alive."

"The fuck, why?"

"I made a promise. Gave him my word. I think he's in trouble."

"Shit, Levon. Any promises you made back then timed out by now. You did your part. You don't owe anybody anything anymore."

"That's not how I see it."

"Yeah. You wouldn't."

"Can you find him?"

"Sure. Sure. One guy in a shithole country that's tearing itself apart every day? A phone call or two and I'll have him for you. Maybe he's on Facebook."

"I figure he's in the fight to retake Mosul. He's with the Kurds or his old militia unit."

"That's so fucking helpful, Levon. It really is."

"You'll do this for me."

"You know I will. You owe *him* something and I owe *you* a shit-ton more. Give me until the end of the week. How do I reach you?"

"I'll call you."

"Friday, Levon. Stay hid till then."

5

Gunny Leffertz said:

"A man doesn't fear what's to come. There's nothing he can do about the future. He fears what he left behind. That's a dogging fear that never leaves."

She got suspicious when her father let her have another Frosty. He never let her have a second Frosty.

Merry came back from the counter to where her father sat at a booth near the front of the Wendy's. He was nursing a coffee and watching the traffic pass by on the Golden Mile. She slid in on the bench opposite and lifted a heaping lump of soft serve from the cup.

"Merry, there's something we need to talk about."

The first mouthful of sweet chocolate turned bitter as chalk in her mouth.

He told her about his friend in Iraq. The promise he

made to the man. The kind of trouble the man and his family were in.

"You really need to go?" she said.

"I do."

"Do you want to go?"

"No, honey. I don't. The very last thing in the world I want is to leave you. But you've got Uncle Fern to look after you until I get back. You'll be so busy taking care of Montana you'll never notice I'm gone."

Montana was the pony he'd bought her. She was devoted to the animal.

"That's not true."

"It's not a deployment. I'll be back once I've helped my friend and I've made sure his family is safe."

"Like you did for us."

"Just like that."

"He's a very good friend?"

"Honest? I wouldn't be here if it wasn't for him. He risked everything to help people who were mostly strangers to him. And he kept on taking those risks. I just cannot turn my back when he needs help."

"Isn't it our government's job to help him if he's our friend?"

"Doesn't work like that, honey. Governments don't keep those kinds of promises to people like my friend."

"Do you know his family?"

"I met his wife once. He had a little girl the same age as you. He had another daughter since I last saw him. Maybe more."

"And they're in trouble?"

"The worst kind, from the worst people on earth. I have to know they're okay. I can't have peace without knowing."

"I'm going to miss you." There were tears in her eyes that she wanted to blame on brain freeze. The Frosty, untouched after the first spoonful, was melting to soup.

"I'm going to miss you too, honey. Miss you every day," he said. He took her hand in his.

"Can we go home now?"

"We sure can. Do you want to take your dessert with you?"

"No. You were right. One is more than enough."

The drive back to Uncle Fern's was a long, silent one for both of them.

6

Gunny Leffertz said:

"You face death with a man, you have a brother for life."

Randall "Duck" Withers was spoiled for life.

He made a promise to himself that he would never, ever fly anything but corporate again.

In the comfortable embrace of a plush leather armchair, with a vodka and tonic on ice in his meaty paw, Duck could barely hear the big jet engines propelling the Airbus over the Atlantic. He had a preseason game between the Dolphins and the Jets up on the big screen. And an attendant was warming up a shrimp creole over rice for him in the galley.

It all beat the living shit out of the days he spent sitting on a bench in the back of a C-130, suffering through another bone-shaking ride to someplace where everyone was looking to shoot his ass off. He was either too cold or too hot back in those days. Today he was jetting to Europe in climate-controlled comfort, and being treated like an oil sheik. The only thing that could move the experience closer to paradise would be a blow job followed by a nap. And, as he'd be landing in Amsterdam inside of the next two hours, both those wishes were within reach.

Duck was Vice President of Operations for Bryson Tactical Services out of Butte, Montana. His job was organizing and running high-security coverage for anyone who could pay the price. And this time the price was over the twenty million mark.

This clusterfuck in Iraq was causing migraines for the oil companies. And in a major way for the Chinese oil giant paying the tab for Duck's team. They wanted boots on the ground and eyeballs on their holdings, as well as protection duty for their personnel and Secret Service level bodyguard coverage for any of their execs visiting in-country. Any ISIS asshole would give up half his virgins and his left nut to grab a big-time oil executive to behead on camera.

The meeting in Amsterdam was to assess the situation and learn what the Chinese expected in return for their euros. Then it would be up to him to put a team together and get them out to the fields in eastern Iraq to help local militias hold on to what hadn't already fallen to the jihadis.

Yeah, he'd come a long way from boot camp at Bragg, where an Army D.I. first called him "Duck" for his unfortunate habit of flinching at loud noises. Determined to lose the nickname, Randy Withers spent more time than any of the recruits out on artillery and mortar ranges. He hung out there, asshole clenched tight, until he could stand in the middle of a barrage without even blinking an eye. The name stuck though, as they always do. Forever he would be Duck. He made it through Ranger school and eventually wound up in Delta. It was there that a CIA wag morphed his sobriquet into 'The Duck of Death.' Duck found it flattering until he saw the Clint Eastwood movie the agency officer had borrowed it from.

Now he lived with it. People knew his name and associated it with a long career of doing bad things to bad people. Inside his world, he was a known man. Through sweat, blood, and two ounces of shrapnel still in his left hip, he made the name Duck synonymous with badass.

He sipped the V & T and took in the scent of the meal heating for him in the galley. Hell, even his Dolphins were winning for once. It just didn't get any better than this.

His sat phone bleated once, twice. He picked it up.

"Go for Withers," he said.

"Took me a while to find you, Duck." The voice on the other end had enough of an easy drawl to take the gruff edge off it. He thought he remembered the voice but told himself that it couldn't be *that* guy.

"Who is this?"

"It's Levon Cade."

The Duck of Death flinched hard, spilling ice from the tumbler into his crotch.

———

"Is this a secure line?" Duck said.

"I'm calling on a cell I bought with cash at a Circle K.

I'm destroying it as soon as we're done talking." Levon's voice even and easy. The man could stand in the fires of hell and never raise his voice.

"You know you're shit hot, right? Everyone I know still in the life is telling me. The stories aren't good."

"I've had some trouble."

"You reaching out to me for cover? I can't do jack for you with domestic law."

"I need to leave the country."

"Uh huh," Duck said. His shrimp creole was congealing into a cold mass in front of him.

"I need to go to Iraq," Levon said.

"You know there's better getaway destinations than that, buddy. Rio. Bali."

"I'm not running. I'm keeping a promise."

"Okay."

"You still have business there. If you don't, you know someone who does. You have a way in for me."

"I have a contract hanging fire now. I'll be putting together a security set-up there sometime next week."

"Put me on the team."

"Hold on there. Levon. I can't put a wanted felon on my crew. Do you know what you're asking me here?"

"Don't bullshit me, Duck. There's no Boy Scouts on your team. You have all the hook-ups. You're the most connected operator I ever ran into. Get me clean ID Passport, visas, and whatever else. Get me in country, and that's the last I'll ask of you."

Duck was sweating despite the chilled air inside the cabin. Cade was asking for a favor without mentioning all the things he'd done for Duck in the past. The man was built that way. He wasn't going to beg, and he wasn't going to mention the overstuffed account in a favor bank with Duck's name on it. And Duck owed him. Owed him big. The big hick had pulled his ass out of more fires than Duck could recall in some of the shittiest places and shittier situations on Earth. That long bad day outside Kabul alone was worth his left kidney, firstborn child, and a weekend in Vegas with his sister.

"I'll need a way to contact you," Duck said finally.

"That's a roger then?"

"Roger."

"I'll contact you on a different cell. We can work out the details. You'll tell me where I need to be and when."

The contact broke. Levon Cade was gone for now.

Duck drained his drink in one long gulp. He gestured for the attendant to take away his untouched plate and wiggled the tumbler for a refill. He sipped at the fresh drink and watched fleecy clouds crawl by below. Levon was keeping a promise. He was into someone else's books for a favor. Duck couldn't imagine that mad Marine ever owing anyone. The Devil's own deal was calling the man back to Iraq.

And Duck knew, sure as he knew the Dolphins would choke in the second half, a whole lot of men would be dead before that promise was kept.

7

"Ed should be back in a few minutes," the chirpy woman behind the desk at the elevators said. "You could wait in his office."

"Are you sure that would be all right?" Nancy Valdez said. She looked to the no-nonsense shield for the ATF hanging on the paneled wall behind the receptionist. Alcohol, Tobacco and Firearms. The T-men. The enforcement wing of the Treasury Department that included Secret Service and the US Marshals.

"Sure. Down this way, and three doors up on your right." The woman pointed.

Edward Bowden's office had only enough room for his desk, chair, a guest chair, and a bookcase bursting with piles of paper. A tall slit window looked out onto a park area enclosed by a section of an aqueduct type of structure that curved around the south end of the building. Everything in the room was standard government issue down to the out-of-date computer. The only personal items in the room were a framed picture of two smiling men squinting in the sun, and an old-fashioned

Mason jar being used as a pen holder. The photo showed an older man with a shrinking fringe of gray hair behind his ears, and a growing roll of fat straining against his suit jacket. The other was a trim young man in the dress blues of the Marine Corps.

"You been waiting long?" A man matching the older man in the photo entered the office. He was perhaps forty pounds lighter than the man in the picture. He set a tall paper cup and a bag from Arby's on the desk.

He had an easy drawl to his voice with a whiskey edge to it. Well-earned in the line of duty, no doubt. In another life he could have made a career doing voice work, selling trucks on TV. Nancy liked him immediately.

"Just got here," she said.

"I treat myself once a week." He nodded to the takeout. "Don't tell my wife. Or my doctor."

"Your secret's safe with me. Nancy Valdez. Special Task Force," Nancy said and stuck out her hand. Ed Bowden took her hand and pressed it firmly in his.

"Ed Bowden. Not-so-special pencil pusher," he said with an open smile. He gestured her to the guest chair.

"You weren't always at a desk," she said. She glanced at the Mason jar.

"I had my time. Sometimes I miss it. Sometimes I wonder what the hell I was thinking." He unpacked his lunch like a practiced ritual. The sandwich sat on the spread-out wrapper upon which he dumped a heap of fries with a squirt of horseradish sauce by it.

"Take a fry or three," he insisted.

Nancy helped herself to one. Salty, greasy, and sinful. She plucked a napkin from the desktop to wipe her hands.

"We're looking for someone who may be hiding out in a hostile environment," she said. Down to business.

"Yeah?"

"He's an Alabama native gone to ground in his home county."

Ed nodded as he took a pull on his shake.

"We know going in we're going to get zero cooperation from the locals. Maybe you could come over to Fifteen Hundred and give us a few pointers."

"I mostly worked Virginia and West Virginia. But I understand the problem you're anticipating. Spent a lot of years dealing with those folks. Hell, they're *my* folks." Now it was Ed's turn to look at the humble jar on his desk. His eyes focused on something far away.

"Could you get away this afternoon?" Nancy said.

"Shit. If I can bring lunch along, we could leave now. I'd wrestle a bear to get away from this office." He began scooping up his lunch to replace it in the bag.

"That works too," Nancy said.

———

"I worked hills and hollers for close to twenty years. Most of that undercover. Making buys. Locating stills," Ed Bowden said. He was addressing Nancy's task force at their conference table inside their quad of cubicles on the fifth floor. Tony Marcoon, Chad Bengstrom and Laura Strand were present along with Nancy.

"Like working a neighborhood in narco," Tony said.

"In some ways, just like that. But in some real important ways, not like that at all," Ed said. "In your inner-city neighborhoods, the drug business ebbs and flows. Shifts in power. Changing customer base. Different product. In all those areas, the whiskey trade is a whole different animal. And all of that is bad news for you."

"How so?" Laura's eyes were large behind her lollypop glasses. She was fascinated with what this old warhorse was schooling them on.

"Well, the power structure is consistent. And I mean for generations, going back a hundred years or more sometimes. And the customer base is always the same. Shot houses up and down the East Coast. Some of these old boys even ship their hooch out to California. Trendy assholes out there sipping white lightning made by rednecks they wouldn't spit on. And the product? Never changes. Same as it's always been. High-octane liquor made out of any shit that'll ferment. You don't want to know what goes into those thumpers."

"And that makes our job of finding our man more difficult," Nancy said.

"A hundred times more. If this Cade is family to folks in the county, they'll never give him up. Hell, they wouldn't give him up if he was their worst enemy. Not to the law. And never to federal revenue agents."

"Revenue agents." Chad, eyes on his open laptop, barked a laugh.

"That's what we are to them. They resent Uncle Sam shutting them down. To them it's a tax issue, a freedom issue. It's not about whiskey. It's about holding on to your own. It's suspicion and pride, is what it is. You could knock on every door and talk yourself hoarse, and not get any closer to this boy than you are right now."

"What do you suggest?" Nancy said.

"Go in sideways. Not undercover, exactly. Find someone who likes to talk. But no suits and badges. Just askin' around," Ed said. He looked around the table with a critical eye: a Latina, an Italian, a Black woman, and a Yankee nerd.

"Guess I just volunteered," Ed said.

Everyone but Chad got it, and chuckled.

"What?" Chad said, looking up from his screen.

8

Gunny Leffertz said:

"Women lie, and soldiers bitch. That's the way of the world."

There were six men on board the Gulfstream when Levon arrived. They sat at the rear of the jet sharing beers and conversation. From the tone of the talk, it was clear they all knew one another well. It was all bullshitting and ball-busting.

"You better take those pills, Mac. You catch every fucking bug."

"Remember that time in Herat? Pukin' and shittin' at the same time?"

"Projectile shitting! Never saw that before."

"What was it? Raisins?"

"Dumb fucker, buying raisins at a souk. You know they weren't washed."

"Shit. They probably weren't raisins."

Levon stowed his bag in the overhead and waited for a lull. He introduced himself, taking note of each man's name. Handshakes and nods all around. Their hands were rough, and their eyes were hard above the open smiles. They assessed him, and found him to be cool until proven otherwise. He was one of their breed, and that was enough. He returned the nods and retreated to a seat a few rows forward. The talk picked up again after the pause. Jabs, counter jabs, and dry laughter.

The jet was an older model due for a refit, showing signs of years of wear and thousands of hours in the air. The upholstery was crushed and stained. The carpet in the aisle was worn down the middle. It still beat military transport all to hell. Quiet ride, snacks, and ice-cold beers.

The co-pilot came along the aisle, assuring them take-off was imminent as he made his way aft to draw the hatch shut. Levon watched workers at the tiny municipal airport roll the steps away from the jet and back to the hangar. The cockpit hatch was open, and he could hear a muted exchange of radio back and forth. The engines spun up to taxi speed. He watched the flat landscape roll past his window, grass dotted with scrub pines. They broke free of the tarmac with a jerk. Within seconds they were banking east, the rooftops and parking lot of a strip mall soaring by below the wingtip. Then neighborhoods of spiral-wound roads and baseball diamonds. Trees took over from there, and the plane tipped out of its cant to fly level through a nearly cloud-less sky.

"This your first private sector gig?"

Levon turned from the window to see a guy holding

out a Coors tallboy to him. Soldier fit and surfer tan. A tattoo in the shape of Helmand province in Afghanistan visible on the inside of his right forearm. The image was bound in loops of barbed wire. His smile was friendly, even as his eyes studied Levon with keen curiosity.

"Yeah. Pays better than Uncle Sammy." Levon accepted the beer. The other man dropped into a seat across the aisle and reached out to clink the neck of his own beer with Levon's.

"Bryson Tac takes care of us. Good pay, benefits. And there's plenty of work for us."

"I'll see how I like it," Levon said.

"Marine, right? You have the walk." The guy leaned on the armrest, nodding.

"Didn't realize there was a walk."

"It was a bullshit guess."

"You nailed it. I'm a jarhead."

"How many times you been down range?"

"Two deployments to Iraq. Three to Afghanistan," Levon lied. He'd lost count of all his deployments and ops to those countries, and a dozen more in both hemispheres.

"Hector Ortiz. Call me Hec." He offered his hand and Levon took it.

"Warren Teller," Levon lied again. Duck Withers' papers were immaculate. Passport, driver's license, social security. Warren Lloyd Teller died in a chopper crash off Coronado Island two years ago. His resurrection would draw no notice, since Levon would never be cashing a Bryson Tactical check.

"Nobody calls him Hector!" one of the men in the rear seats called out.

"His name's 'Butterknife'!" called another.

"Fuck you," Hector said. A wincing grin. He turned back to Levon.

"We were on a roadblock on Highway One in Helmand. We were searching through the back of a truck, and I got a little too handsy with some haji mama. I found the brown heroin cakes she was hiding under her burkha."

"He found everything!" one of the men shouted.

"But her knife!" the others sang out in chorus.

Hector lifted his polo shirt to show a jagged line of scar tissue across the flesh under his ribs. He smiled crooked and shrugged.

"What happened to her?" Levon said.

"Shit, I hope she's *still* sitting in Pul-e-Charkhi. I was down for close to a year before I got back. I almost needed a colostomy bag, for Christ's sake."

"What's the duty like when we land? What's our job?" Levon wanted to move off war stories. He wasn't ready to share any of his.

"Security, mostly. We guard the SinoChem compound. Ride shotgun for execs and visitors when they visit the oil fields. It's all in the Al-Muthanna, far away from the clusterfuck with ISIS. A pizza run, mostly."

"Why did a Chinese oil company hire an American security firm?"

"The Chinese keep a low profile in the region. It's like they're not even there. No corporate logos visible. They like their gun hands to be Westerners in case there's a fuck-up. No Chinese faces on CNN. No bad press."

"So it's quiet."

"It's boring. Drives in the desert and nights binge-watching Netflix. The Chinese have a nice gym on the compound though. But no need for the beard, brother. Nothing covert."

"I'll shave when I get there," Levon said. He ran a hand through the week-long growth already dense on his jaws and chin.

Hector continued doing most of the talking for the next hour as they left the sun far behind them and the sky grew darker. He told Levon that he washed out of Ranger school once and the sniper school at Benning twice. He resigned himself to being an infantry grunt and pulled four deployments in Afghanistan before deciding he wanted to stop fighting for a bunch of ungrateful hajis and start fighting for himself.

"Not much action though. Last time I fired my weapon was to scatter a herd of goats that were blocking a motorcade," he said.

"There's a lot to be said for not getting shot at," Levon said.

"Hey, you probably want to get some sleep instead of listening to me bitch. See you on the ground, okay?" Hector pushed up out of the seat. He fist-bumped Levon and returned to his pals snoozing in the back.

"Yeah. You can show me around the compound," Levon lied once more.

Once his boots hit the ground he'd be gone, bound for Mosul.

9

"Been gettin' much rain this fall?" Ed Bowden said. He was talking to a girl behind the counter at a six-stool place called Fay's in some blow-through town called Colby.

"You a farmer?" the girl said. She was pouring fresh ground coffee into a paper filter.

"Not so much these days," he said.

"Didn't think so with those hands." She smiled, not meaning it as a criticism.

"Been in sales since I left home. Feed corn, machines. Still in farming in a way, I suppose."

"What brings you to Colby?" She was struggling to fix the coffee receptacle into an ancient drop machine. It slid home with a clank.

"My wife's niece, guess that makes her my niece too. We came down from Charlotte for her wedding. Staying all week."

"In Colby? Maybe I know her."

"Nah. Over in Haley. I told them I needed to gas up the car and slipped on out."

"Long way to come for gas."

"I had to get away from all those hens cackling."

She laughed at that. A high titter that ended in a sweet sigh.

"Then stay for a refill," she said. She tipped a coffee pot to top him off.

Ed never thought he'd be in the field again. They'd shifted him over to a desk for the last eight years to his twenty. And here he was undercover again. Not the kind of undercover that had him waking up in a cold sweat like back in the day. He was Terrence Riggins now, with a driver's license, insurance, Legion card, and Mastercard to prove it. Instead of meeting under the moonlight on lonely roads to trade dollars for whiskey, he was nosing around little flyspeck towns like this making small talk.

There were a few thousand Cades in the state, and a hundred or more in this county. He could spend what was left of his life and never get a whiff of the man he was looking for. Chad Bengstrom worked up some search theories for him utilizing a system the US Navy used to hunt for missing submarines back in the 1960s and '70s. Chad looked at incidences of violent crime across the entire state of Alabama. According to what Nancy and her team told him about the man they sought, unexplained homicides followed this Levon Cade like fleas after a dog. Using his submarine search program, Chad found a dense cluster of possibly related murders, unidentified corpses, arson and theft in this county. The thickest collection of incidents was right here, within a ten-mile-wide radius of this little one-gas-station town.

Hard to reconcile that with what he could see

through the front glass of Fay's. A two-lane with only the occasional pickup drifting past. A gas station and an ice cream place shuttered now for the winter. The sign out front read: CL SED TIL SUM ER.

He knew that the real heart of this place was the hills that rose up either side of the road, and the hollers and deeps hidden down between the ridgelines that marched away to the horizon. It was all changed from his day. His job was all administrative now. Making sure the proper forms were applied to the proper cases. But it still brought him in frequent contact with active ATF agents and US Marshals.

When he walked hills like this, the *same* damned hills in a different state, he sniffed the air for mash, or looked for runs of PVC pipes up from crick beds that drew the water to thirsty stills. Even the sound of a chainsaw could mean someone had a thumper close by. Stills needed a steady supply of firewood too.

Now, so they told him, it was mostly meth being cooked in these woods. In his time, there were some bad actors who distilled with ingredients not meant for consumption. Pine needles, sawdust. One fella he caught was using pig shit to speed the process. Liquor that would make you permanently blind. But most of the old boys up here took pride in their product, and used only the freshest water and clean mash.

Not the same for meth. There was no wrong way to make that shit, and almost all the ingredients were lethal. It was just evil stuff. Made anyone who used it bat-shit crazy, and that included the assholes making it. Ed met very few shiners who were drunks. But all these drug folks were tainted by their product.

He reminded himself to step lightly. The old suspicions of outsiders still lingered over these hills. He'd been out driving these roads, stopping at roadside BBQ wagons, Legion halls, feed stores, and anywhere else locals might be found. In the past few weeks, he'd gotten nowhere—either blank stares or a sly change of subject. Lots of times, whoever he was talking to would simply walk away.

"So, are you Fay?" he said. The pretty girl behind the counter was busy at the sink washing cups. Not too busy to offer another of her smiles.

"That was my mama named the place. But I'm Fay too."

"That would make you a junior if you were a boy. Not sure what that makes a girl having the same name as her mother."

"Well, she's gone now so it's just me."

"Sorry to hear that. Bet she'd be proud of you keeping this place up so nice."

"Maybe."

She set the cups on a tray to dry. Ed took a sip of coffee. Fay broke the silence.

"What's your niece's last name? I mean her maiden name. I might not know her, but I bet I know her family."

"Cade. Elizabeth Cade."

Fay's smile returned.

"I know some Cades live close by here."

10

Gunny Leffertz said:

"They say a jarhead has no home. Not so. A Marine is home anywhere he can dig a hole and point a rifle."

The sun had sunk below the faraway horizon hours before. Baking heat still radiated from the runway surface despite the fresh chill in the air.

Levon joined the other men in an MRAP vehicle waiting at the edge of the field. They loaded in their luggage and climbed on board. The big transport truck bore no markings. Levon noted it was Chinese made.

"Thought you said it was quiet here. Why all the armor?" Levon asked Hector as they took seats on the benches lining either wall of the MRAP's interior.

"The Chinese play it safe. You know what it's like here. One minute everything's cool, and the next the kid who sold you a Coke yesterday is firing an RPG at your hotel room," Hector said.

Levon nodded.

Away from the lights of the airfield, the only breaks in the pitch darkness were the winking red marker lights atop the slant drill rigs set far off the road surface to either side. The road away from the airfield curved up an incline toward a false green-hued dawn of halogen lights that illuminated SinoChem's employee compound.

The armored transport slowed to pass through a gap in a ten-foot earth berm that ringed the compound. The MRAP wormed through a maze of Jersey barriers before coming to a full stop in front of a guard bunker fortified with sand-filled HESCO barriers. The HESCO was a wire mesh and heavy-duty fabric box the size of a refrigerator. They could be filled with dirt, sand, or gravel to make quick-fix bunkers and embrasures. Uniformed men came out. After a few words shared with the driver, they waved the transport through.

Levon looked through the slit of a viewport, a view distorted by the inches of angled ballistic glass. He noted that all the guards appeared to be Westerners. They wore no unit markings though their BDUs and their web gear were of uniform issue. The compound itself bore no identification other than a white steel sign that announced this place as Site A-9 in English, French, and Arabic. Missing was a translation in Chinese characters.

They rolled along a paved road through a collection of buildings that looked like a modern college campus transported to a desert. The transport deposited them before a row of modular buildings set back off a road across a yard of raked sand that was enclosed by a border of white-washed stones. All very chickenshit G.I. and orderly.

The unit off the plane were met by a company employee, the first Chinese national they encountered since beginning their journey. In his slacks, boat shoes, and windbreaker he looked like the entertainment director on a cruise ship. He introduced himself as James and spoke flawless English tinged with an Oxford accent.

He gave them a short introductory orientation, welcoming back anyone returning, even making a joke about round eyes all looking alike. A few of the guys chuckled politely. The rest had heard the joke before. He cautioned them not to drink alcohol this evening, as they would be on duty at first light. He wished them a good night and departed.

Inside the modular building, the air was comfortably dry. There was a great room with steel cages for their gear lining the walls. Full complements of weapons, web gear, body armor, and ammo. All either new or reconditioned. Each man was assigned his own dorm room with a bunk, dresser, and wardrobe. Flatscreen TV on the wall and a mini fridge. Inside the wardrobe were two sets of clean BDUs, ball caps, and boots identical to those worn by the guards. No insignia. The labels inside read "Made in China."

The whole structure showed signs of previous occupants, remnants of tape where photos were placed on paneled walls, but every surface was recently wiped clean. He set his bag atop the bunk and sat down on the edge of the mattress. It was the most comfortable billet Levon had ever seen. He almost regretted that he wouldn't be staying.

Hector appeared in his doorway.

"We don't get orders till the morning. The rest of us are going over for pizza and Cokes. You coming?" he said.

"I'll be along," Levon said. "I just want to square myself away here."

"Sure. The Pizza Hut's kitty corner from here. Just head right to the main road. It's along on the left at the back of the parking lot."

"Roger that," Levon said.

Hector was gone from the door, calling out to someone down the corridor.

Levon waited until he heard the voices retreat and the door to the outside slam. He could feel the quiet all around but for the hum of the air-conditioning. He was alone.

In the floor of his gear bag was a false bottom. Inside was a packet of documents sealed in plastic. Duck Withers had provided it. Marching orders and the ID that would get him off the base with transport. After that he was on his own. After that it was terra incognita.

He slit the packet open with his clasp knife. He read the specs on his new ID, memorizing the data. He stuffed the papers into a pocket of his jacket. In the great room, he found the call-out cage with his name on it. Or Warren Teller's name. He found a heavy canvas gear bag and loaded it with an oil-shiny M4 rifle, twenty magazines, a Browning automatic and three magazines, a half dozen frag grenades, and a med pack. He left behind the body armor and boots and the rest of the web gear.

He transferred plastic-wrapped bundles of cash from the false bottom of his carry-on bag into the pouches of his new ruck. A desert tan Orca backpack. The rest of the contents of his carry-on—change of socks, under-wear, clasp knife and butane lighter—went into pouches on the backpack. Before stowing the bundles of cash, he slit a pack open and drew out a stack of twenties he folded in half and stuck in his shirt pocket. He humped it all outside, backpack, rifle, and gear bag.

Instead of turning right as Hector suggested, Levon made his way left toward a dark lot where a row of cars waited. One of them was a ten-year-old 4Runner with a sun-bleached paint finish that was once pewter. The windshield was cracked down the center. He opened the driver door and lifted the floor mat. An ignition key lay in the dust just as Duck promised. The Toyota whined to life, and he steered it back the way they'd come toward the gate.

At the gate the guard examined the papers Levon offered him. The guard was an Aussie who narrowed his eyes to study Levon's face.

"You lot just got here, mate," he said.

"No rest for the wicked. The home office called. I got to run this errand ASAP." Levon managed a smile and a shrug.

"You know the way?"

"I'll find it. Just follow the road, right? Not like I could get lost."

"Nothing but wall-to-wall fuck-all out there," the Aussie said and waved him through.

The gates swung upward. Levon piloted around the barriers and out into the enveloping black.

11

It wasn't the first time revenue agents had been in the valley. But never in such force. This was an invading army.

A convoy of unmarked trucks came from either end of the county road in the hours before dawn. They were met by county sheriff cars and state police cruisers where a two-lane curved around the foot of a wooded hill. The entrance to a dirt road lay nearly invisible in the brush. The locals and staties were waiting outside their vehicles, shotguns and AR-15s slung atop chest armor. No different than opening day of hunting, waiting in the twilight for the sun to peep over the ridgetop.

They were having breakfast from take-out containers laid atop the hoods of the cars—a hillbilly buffet.

The government trucks pulled to a stop along the verges. Men in body armor and ballistic helmets climbed from the rear of the vehicles. The staties eyed them with suspicion. The locals looked at the weaponry the feds were sporting with open lust. Rail systems fitted with gear that looked like they came from a Star Wars movie.

The ATF agents and US Marshals saw the noshing cops as a medieval knight might see a serf armed with a pole; useful, so long as they didn't get in the way.

With the trucks was an unmarked government car. Nancy Valdez exited with Laura Strand and Tony Marcoon walking behind. They wore chest armor and Treasury windbreakers. Their badges swung on lanyards from their necks. Nancy was the highest-ranking agent here, and it was her operation start to finish. But she knew to defer to the professional hard chargers. She stood listening as Agent Parks approached the locals.

The leader of the combined team of tactical feds, a Black man with a professional smile, towered over the state police captain.

"Special Agent Lester Parks. I want to thank you for coming out this morning," the tall Black man said to the captain and the group at large.

"Captain Brett Poteet, Alabama's finest. How can I be of assistance, sir?" the smaller man said.

Parks told the captain to spread his men along the road for a distance of a quarter mile each direction and to listen to the assigned radio frequency. Parks would use this to keep them updated. Their job was to watch for their suspect, in the distant eventuality that he made it through the cordon of feds to the roadway. Photos of Levon Cade, blurry ones from a surveillance camera, were distributed to all the officers. Parks addressed the cops crowded around him while his team spread out to begin the climb through the woods.

"This Cade is supposed to be some kind of badass jarhead. He will be armed. And he is damned dangerous. Now, your government wants him alive. But don't take any chances. If this guy draws on you, you drop him.

Drop him hard. And put two more in him once he's dropped. Do not underestimate this man. I cannot stress that enough. That said, make damn sure of your targets. I'd like to go home to my wife myself."

That drew chuckles from a couple of staties. The county cops wore frozen expressions, wondering how the hell they got into this one.

"I like to keep everyone informed. What we're doing is approaching the house up this drive. Both from the road, and with a second unit already staged atop the hill to prevent flight that way. In all likelihood, we'll have this guy in custody inside the hour. But it's good to know you men have our backs in case this asshole gets lucky."

Parks noticed a female deputy blinking at him.

"Men *and* women at our backs. Good to see you all," he said.

The female deputy beamed back an embarrassed smile.

"Thanks to all of you, and let's make this a good morning," Parks said. He trotted up the hill to follow the line of men ascending into the naked trees. He was out of sight in seconds.

The state police captain directed his forces to move out along the road at intervals. He remained by his cruiser, the one that was serving as an impromptu banquet table. Nancy introduced her team.

"What did this guy do?" the captain said.

"We're still making a list," Nancy said.

———

Uncle Fern woke to the hounds barking. He levered himself up in the recliner where he'd fallen asleep the night before watching a John Wayne movie on the TV. Feller, the ridgeback, rose to approach the front door, ears up and hairs along its spine standing straight. The hounds went silent.

He was rising out of the chair when the front door crashed in. The door at the back of the house caved at the same time. The ridgeback leaped and got batted aside by a ballistic shield on the arm of the first man through the door. The biggest man Fern had ever seen in his seventy years. Another man applied a stun gun to Feller's neck. The dog dropped, twitching as though in a waking dream. The big man was followed in by a phalanx of shouting men who spread out into the house, weapons up and shoving furniture aside.

Fern got to his feet with three gun barrels pointed his way. He waved them off to turn to the dog lying still in the corner. Gloved hands were on him and pushed him hard to the floor. His wrists were zip-tied behind him.

"If you hurt Feller, you'll wish you were never born," Fern said from the corner of his mouth, his face pressed to the threadbare carpet.

"Dog's okay, old man. Just stunned."

"You have a warrant for this?"

"Chief, we got so many warrants they needed a truck to haul them all. District judge got a hand cramp signing them."

From all over the house came shouts of "Clear! Clear! Clear!" Boots tramped overhead. Furniture crashed to the floor. Boots on the porch.

"Stable building's clear, sir! Carport too!"

"Sweep the whole place. Watch for hides in the woods above us," the enormous Black man said.

Hands lifted Fern to his feet and guided him to the kitchen, where he was planted in a chair at his own kitchen table.

"Where's your nephew?" the Black man said.

"Beats the shit out of me." Fern shrugged.

———

The marshals and ATF men were grid searching the woods and clearings around the Cade property. Even if they didn't find the man, there was work to be done. They'd be here for days tearing the place apart for evidence. And more.

"Nice truck outside. Yours?" Nancy said.

"Yeah," Fern said, peering at her from the corners of his eyes. He was un-cuffed with a mug of coffee on the table before him. There was a box of donuts Nancy had carried up from the gaggle of cop cars down the hill.

"Is that a four-wheel drive? The Silverado is nice, huh?"

"Are my dogs all right?" Fern could hear them howling somewhere back of the house.

"They're okay. The goat too. We got them leashed up," Tony Marcoon said from where he leaned back against the kitchen sink.

"How'd you buy that truck?" Nancy said.

"Same's anyone else. On time," Fern said. He straightened in his seat to look her dead on.

"Says here you paid cash." Nancy swiped the screen of a pad with a manicured finger. "Fully loaded package. All-wheel. Air. Leather seats. Set you back close to $60k."

Fern said nothing.

"You want to tell me how you covered that with your social security and veteran disability checks?"

Fern looked away.

"One phone call and I can start a process that ends with you losing this cabin and property along with that truck and anything else you own. Have you ever had an audit? Ever danced with the taxman?"

Laura Strand entered the kitchen, glanced at the tired old man slumped now in a chair.

"There's a room upstairs with all kinds of girl stuff in it. Clothes. Stuffed animals," she said.

Nancy stood to come around the table beside Fern. She leaned in close to study his eyes.

"That's right. Your grandniece. Can you tell us where we can find Meredith Cade? Merry, right?" Nancy smiled easy, head tilted.

Fern turned to look at her, his gaze filled with fire.

12

The 4Runner gave up just after dawn.

The engine knocked and kicked with a fury. Steam scented with the sweet odor of boiled coolant billowed from under the hood. Levon pulled to the sandy verge of the string-straight two-lane. The engine went into a final, and mortal, seize.

Three hours till noon, and the air was already furnace hot. He waved away flies and popped the hood. A geyser of steam erupted from a burst pipe, making him step back or be scalded. A greenish-brown puddle grew in the sand under his feet. The Toyota was bleeding out from a dozen blown gaskets.

He popped the rear hatch and pulled the Orca pack and the gear bag onto the dropped tailgate. He stripped naked but for his socks and tossed his Western clothes into a ditch along the roadside. He was in no danger of being seen. There was nothing but flat sand and rock for miles in every direction. He'd passed no traffic on the way from the SinoChem compound either coming or going. From the Orca, he pulled out worn cotton clothes.

Loose fitting pants, a pair of Russian-issue light duty boots, a plaid buttoned shirt, knockoff YSL jacket, and a keffiyeh in a fine checked pattern. He kept the rifle and ammo in the gear bag, but secured the Browning in his waistband at the small of his back. He checked his look in the side mirror. With the keffiyeh in place along with a pair of Ray-Ban knockoffs and a good start on a beard, he wouldn't rate a second glance at a distance.

Levon popped the top of a gallon jug of water from a case stowed in the rear of the Toyota. He drank a little more than a quart, until his belly was filled with water. He held the remainder over his head to douse himself with the contents. He slung the pack on his back and the gear bag over his shoulder, and hefted a gallon jug of water to carry in each hand before setting out west along the endless ribbon of road.

————

It was past three in the afternoon by his expert appraisal of the sun's position high in the yellow sky. He'd finished half of one of the gallon jugs and was perspiring it away faster than he could replace it. Thin trails of vapor rose from his sweat-soaked clothing.

There was no shade anywhere around. The next settlement along the road was at least a full day's hike. He could do another twenty miles before it turned full dark. He'd camp cold somewhere off the road. Very cold. The desert could drop to freezing at night. Colder if there was a wind. He set his eyes ahead and marched, a cadence he learned at Pendleton to keep time.

They say that in the Marine Corps

the pay is mighty fine,
they give you a hundred dollars
and take back ninety-nine.
Oh Lord, I wanna go,
but they won't let me go,
no oh oh oh oh oh oh oh. Hey!!

They say that in the Marine Corps;
the chow is mighty fine,
a roll fell off the table,
and killed a friend of mine.
Oh Lord I wanna go,
but they won't let me go,
no oh oh oh oh oh oh oh. Hey!!

They say that in the Marine Corps;
the bunks are mighty fine,
but how the hell would they know,
they never slept in mine.
Oh Lord I wanna go,
but they won't let me go,
no oh oh oh oh oh oh oh. Hey!!

They say that in the Marine Corps;
the coffee is mighty fine,
looks like muddy water,
and tastes like turpentine.
Oh Lord I wanna go,
but they won't let me go,
no oh oh oh oh oh oh oh. Hey!!

He lost count of the rounds he chanted under his breath as he humped along the roadway. The skillet heat rose up through the neoprene soles of the Russian desert boots. He added verses he remembered about the women, food, and fun that the Corps promised to enlistees.

The voice of his first D.I., a mean-as-a-snake gunny named Bromwell came to him in his imagination. "Barfin'" Bromwell was the name one platoon of greenies after another had graced him with. Nothing pleased Gunny Bromwell more than the sight of his recruits puking their guts up after a forced march with full packs on a ten-mile run. The man rejoiced in vomit and would offer commentary on the smell, trajectory, and color of the spew exploding from the pogues under this command.

Levon's shadow grew longer behind him as the sun turned orange and then red and drooped toward the horizon. He stopped to drain the last of his first jug of water. The next would have to last him the rest of the next day. Levon turned to pitch the empty jug off the road. He saw a plume of white against the darkening sky to the east. He stood in the center of the road and watched the plume grow, and beneath it, a dark shape appeared. The vehicle was small in the distance, tiny enough to be covered by the tip of his little finger and then his middle finger and then his thumb. He moved to the sand along the verge as the vehicle took on a distinct shape in the wavering heat rising off the road surface.

There was nowhere to conceal himself. He stood and waited as the truck rolled closer, finally come to a stop a hundred yards from where he stood. Levon's hand moved to the butt of the handgun at his back. His gear bag lay open at his feet by the remaining gallon jug. The M4 lay inside fully charged with a round in the spout.

The Toyota HiLux was battered and scored. The official transport of practically every jihadist on the planet. He couldn't see if it mounted a gun in the back. There were no passengers visible in the truck bed. The reflection of the setting sun off the windshield turned the glass to a mirror.

With a puff of blue exhaust, the HiLux started forward. Levon stood his ground but for a single step back away from the roadside. The pickup pulled to a stop alongside him, engine ticking. A grinning face regarded him from behind the steering wheel.

"You look like you could use a ride, Levon Cade," said Hector Ortiz. His grin grew wider at Levon trying to hide any trace of surprise.

13

The cow was smiling, really smiling—a big sloppy grin under big lazy eyes.

"Saw it when I was bringing them in for milking," Randy Eslinger said. "Never seen a cow so happy to get milked."

"Do you have bolt cutters?" Jessie Hamer said.

"In the shed," Randy said.

"You better get them," Jessie said.

Jessie and Merry waited while Randy moved at his own speed, slow, toward a leaning wooden shed just off the barn. Merry stood by the dusty white dairy cow in the barnyard, patting its neck.

"What happened to her?" Merry said.

"I'm betting she got into Mr. Eslinger's compost pile. I saw this once when I was in veterinary school," Jessie said.

"What would a cow eat to make it smile?"

"You'll see in a minute."

It was more like five minutes as Randy banged around in the shed looking for those cutters. He emerged eventually with a pair of long-handled bolt cutters and ambled back their way.

Merry cooed while Randy did his best to hold the cow's mouth open.

"Ho, girl. The lady's just here to help," Randy cooed in the twitching ear.

The big bovine lowed and snorted. Merry had to dance around to avoid stomping hooves. Jessie worked the blades of the bolt cutter into the cow's mouth. She maneuvered them around at the angle she wanted before drawing the handles together. Something in the cow's mouth crunched then popped. Two halves of a long section of watermelon rind dropped to the dirt.

"That's it. Essie's back to her usual enigmatic expression," Jessie said.

Randy led the cow back toward a gate and out to a field where her sisters stood along the fence watching the show.

"That's it?" Merry said.

"Sometimes it's simple as that. A watermelon rind stuck in sideways. I'll have to tell Mr. Eslinger to fence in that compost dump."

They walked to the pickup truck decorated with the prancing horse symbol of Riverstone Veterinary. Jessie removed her gloves and tossed them on the dash. They waited for Randy's return.

"Doesn't Sandy ever come out on your route with you?" Merry said. Sandy was Jessie's daughter.

"She has school and all. And boys. And I guess she's at that age when hanging out with your mom's just not cool anymore."

"Teenagers," Merry said.

"Aren't you one now?"

"I don't feel like one."

"You will."

Randy made his way back to them across the barnyard.

"What do I owe you, Jessie?"

"What do you think it was worth?"

"Twenty?" Randy said.

"Done."

Randy dug in his jeans and came up with some wrinkled bills that Jessie folded and stuck in the pocket of her work shirt. She gave the farmer a warning about securing his compost before climbing into the cab.

"Will you ever be going back to school?" Jessie said. She piloted the F-150 down the drive away from the farm.

"Can't see how. Daddy says we're laying low." Merry held a hand out the window, fingers joined in a wedge to feel the lift and drag of the air over them.

"You'll be getting further behind."

"I probably learned more today with you than I would have sitting in a classroom."

"Sure, cutting melons out of dumb cows' pieholes."

"And I been reading all of Uncle Fern's books."

"And what do you learn from them?"

"You can ask me almost any question about the Marines and I bet I can answer it," Merry said.

The rode in silence along a tree-shaded lane. The leaves were turning color. The road surface was carpeted with a riot of shapes in warm shades that were sent swirling as they passed.

"Have you heard from your father?" Jessie said.

"No. He said I probably wouldn't for a while," Merry said. She counted mailboxes as they passed.

"It's okay to miss him. I do. It's all right to feel sad."

Merry said nothing for four mailboxes.

"He *had* to go," she said. Quiet voice.

"He did, honey."

When they arrived at the entry to Riverstone, they were met by state troopers walking to them from a pair of cruisers parked in the grass by the end of the drive.

14

Gunny Leffertz said:

"Take your friends where you find them. And watch your ass."

"You went over the fence in a goddamn hurry," Hector Ortiz said as he piloted them along the ribbon of concrete.

Levon watched the desert pass by, the sand silver in the moonlight.

"I said to myself, 'fuck it.' Get a good night's sleep and a big breakfast before taking off after your ass." Hector was enjoying himself.

"Why didn't Duck tell me about you?" Levon said.

"'Cause he knew you'd run off just like you did. He said you're some kind of lone wolf. But you're going to need help."

"And that's you?"

"Mr. Withers doesn't want any more direct contact with you. That's my job. I'm your handler. I'm a cut-out."

"Handler."

"You're going to need help. You really think you're going to find this Kurd you're looking for in this shitstorm?"

"He's a Yazidi."

"Yeah. Well, he's with a Kurd unit. Did you know that? Unh-uh. You didn't. That's what I'm here for. To keep you wired in. You know how many Bazît Hassans there are in Iraq? Like Chans in a Chinese phonebook, that's how many."

"Where is Bazît?"

"Right in the middle of the clusterfuck. Place called Gog Jallah, east of Mosul."

"Gogjali."

"You know it?"

"I spent some time there."

Hector snorted and threw his head back to bark a laugh.

"Withers sketched you out for me. You're some kind of shadow legend. I never heard him talk about anyone like he talks about you. Let's just say he's a fan. No details, sure. He says your whole life is classified. They bag your turds and lock them in a safe under the Pentagon."

Levon sipped from a water bottle.

"What's this guy to you? This Bazît," Hector said.

"We fought alongside one another. I made him a promise. I'm here to keep it."

"What was the promise?"

"That nothing would happen to his family."

"Shit! That's not your promise to keep. That's the President's promise."

"It was my personal word."

"Listen, you know better than me that the Kurds and Yazidis have been getting fucked over ever since oil was found here. Before that even. They can never catch a break. You think by now they'd know they're being bull-shitted."

"I didn't bullshit."

"You are one Old Testament motherfucker, Levon Cade. But if you're so set on getting to Mosul, I'll *take* you to Mosul," Hector said.

"You figure three days to get there?" Levon said.

"Two if we share driving. What kind of music you like?" Hector leaned from the wheel to touch an iPod set in a dock on the dash.

"Old school country."

"This is going to be a long drive." Hector sighed.

15

"Do you need anything? Would you like another Coke?" Nancy Valdez said. She stepped into the interrogation room, a folder thick with papers in her arm.

"I'm fine. When can I go home?" Merry said.

She tapped a tattoo on the empty soda can held between her fingers. The room they were in was windowless, practically a cell. A vent in the ceiling hummed, a steady fall of chilled air dropping from it. Everyone had been nice to her. The police on the long ride to the state police barracks. The older grandma-type lady who took her name at one of the desks out front. And this pretty lady who told Merry that she came all the way from Washington to ask Merry some questions.

"We'll talk about that later," Nancy said. She introduced herself and showed Merry her badge and photo ID. She removed a digital recorder from the pocket of her jacket and set it in the middle of the table. She recited her name, the date, time and Merry's full name and date of birth.

"Where is your father?" Nancy said.

"I don't know," Merry said. She looked the Treasury agent in the eyes as her father taught her. She wasn't lying. She had no idea where Levon was.

"Do you mean you don't know where he is right now, or you have no idea where he was going when he left?"

"Either. Both. It's both."

"He didn't tell you he was leaving or where he was going?"

"No, ma'am. I woke up one day and he was gone." That was a lie. She kept her eyes steady.

"And you haven't heard from him since."

"No." True.

"Where do you think he might be? Do you have any ideas?"

Merry shrugged.

"I need a spoken answer." Nancy nodded at the recorder.

"My daddy was a Marine. He used to be gone a long time lots of times. I never asked him where he was going or when he would be back."

"You think he's been deployed?"

"Maybe."

"He hasn't been deployed. Your father has been discharged from service for years and currently holds no rank or any association with the Marines, or any other branch of the military service or any government agency."

"Might be a secret mission."

"We'll get back to that," Nancy said. "We have evidence that your father is in possession of stolen property. Mostly a lot of money stolen from various places that both of you have visited together."

"We only took from bad people. We only took what we needed," Merry said.

"That still makes your father a thief."

"My daddy's not a thief."

"What do you call someone who steals?"

"It wasn't theirs to begin with. And we needed it more than them."

"Is that something your father told you?"

"No, ma'am. That's something I'm saying on my own."

"So, we agree that your father came into possession of money that was not his own. Can you tell me where any of this money is?"

"No, I can't."

"Can't or won't?"

"Both, ma'am."

"Have you seen your father with a disc of some kind? Like a CD disc?"

"No, ma'am."

"Do you know what a flash drive is? A thumb drive?"

"Yes."

"Have you seen your father with anything like that?"

"No, ma'am."

Nancy dropped that line of questioning to open the folder before her. She slid photographs across the table for Merry to look at. Some of them were morgue photos of men obviously dead. For the sake of the recorder, Nancy read off the names of the men as they were written on the backs of the photos.

"Delbert Mathers."

"Louis Jennings Bragg."

"Merle Lee Hogue."

"James Roy Mathers."

Merry did her best to make her face an unmoving mask as, one by one, the pictures were placed before her like a deck of cards.

"Gary Thomas Bush."

"Nelson Clark Granger."

"Donald MacKenzie Fenton."

Merry wanted to look away at that one but held her eyes fixed on the table. That long Maine night in the snow. Poor Mr. Fenton. She felt sad for Carl and Giselle, left without a dad.

"Wolodymyr Kolinsky."

"Danya Kolinsky."

"Vanko Kolinsky."

"Calvin Douglas Shepherd."

The last was a mug shot of another face she knew. The man was older when she saw him in the little diner on a rainy night somewhere in Virginia. Her father left her to follow the man outside, then returned alone. They drove away in a car owned by the man in the picture.

Nancy set down a new series of photos without providing a name for each. They were more morgue photos. Eyes glassy. Mouths slack. Merry recognized one. She saw him die in the snow on the lot of a general store on a lonely road far away in Maine.

Next Nancy laid down a high school picture of a pretty girl smiling, loose curls fell to the shoulders of a crisp white blouse.

"Jenna Marie Wiley."

Then another photo. A smiling woman was squinting into the sunlight where she was seated on the bench at the rear of a pleasure boat. Diamonds of light coming off lake water behind her. At this one Merry clamped her lips tight to contain a gasp.

"Your grandmother." Nancy was done with her little card show. Three rows of ten photos each lay neatly arranged before Merry.

Merry mutely eyed them. If this was a game, she didn't know the rules.

"Do you know what all of these people have in common?"

"No, ma'am."

"They all were, in one way or another, associated with your father, and they are all dead."

Merry said nothing.

Nancy sighed, closing her folder, but allowing the photos to remain where they were.

"Your father has not been the best parent for you. Not a good father. He has made you part of his actions, his crimes. He has placed you in danger by these actions. Do you understand that?"

"My daddy loves me." Merry promised herself, her father, and Jesus that she would not cry. She willed her heart to stone.

"I suppose that he does, in his way, love you. That doesn't change that he has been negligent, even reckless, in your upbringing."

Merry kept her eyes leveled on the Treasury agent's face.

"You're the one who can end this. You can tell me where your father is, and we can resolve all of this."

"You want the money."

It was Nancy's turn to be taken aback. Not only this little girl's words, but the way she stated them. Merry Cade's tone was one of *accusation*. Nancy abandoned the pretense of a friendly tone. She put on the voice she used in court.

"There are federal funds involved here, money involved in criminal enterprise that needs to be confiscated."

"Well, I don't know where anything you want is. My daddy. The money. Or a disc. Or anything. I don't know anything because my daddy didn't tell me anything."

"Then you will not cooperate."

"I can't tell you what I don't know. You can call that not cooperating if you like, ma'am."

"I guess we're done here," Nancy said. She tabbed the recorder to off. She raked the photos back to her and began inserting them back into the folder.

"Can I go home then?" Merry said.

"No. You can't. You're a minor with an absent parent and without a legally assigned guardian."

"What does that mean?" A thrill of panic shot through Merry's stomach, a pinching sensation that made her catch her breath.

"It means you have no family and will be remanded to foster care."

"Uncle Fern is family," Merry said. She stood as Nancy stood.

"That man is not a fit substitute for a parent. He's currently under federal investigation himself and being held as a witness."

"Witness? To what?"

"Wait here. Someone will be in for you." Nancy breezed from the room, the file held tight to her chest.

Out in the CID squad room, Nancy nodded to a woman with a lemony expression seated in the guest, or suspect, chair in front of a detective's desk. The woman rose to enter the interrogation room, a file of her own in her hand.

Nancy Valdez joined Tony Marcoon and Laura Strand in a surveillance room. The two had been sharing a pizza and coffees gone cold now. They'd been watching Nancy at work with the Cade girl, visible on a bank of monitors set on the wall.

"Did you notice her tell? Every time she was lying, she called me 'ma'am,'" Nancy said.

Laura looked at Nancy a second through her lollypop lenses before returning her gaze to the screens where the little girl was crying as the lemon faced woman read to her from a paper set atop the table.

"Jesus Christ, Nance," Marcoon said.

16

Gunny Leffertz said:

"Give a man a fish, he'll eat for a day. Teach a man to fish, and he'll eat every day. Give a man a gun, and he'll make you fish for him."

"Fucking heat," Hector said. "My ball sack feels like it's down around my knees." He pulled himself up using the steering wheel to lift off the seat. He tugged the damp cloth of his pants out of his ass crack.

He waved away a cloud of biting flies that had invaded the truck cab. "Fucking bugs, man."

Levon rode in silence by him.

"Don't you ever bitch, Cade?" Hector said.

"Doesn't do any good."

"Sure, it does. It's good to vent. Soldiers been bitchin' and pukin' since they were in sandals."

"All it does is remind me how miserable I am. Better to talk about anything else."

"Okay. You watch *Game of Thrones?*"

"Is that some kind of quiz show?" Levon said.

"You follow sports?"

"Not since high school."

"You don't know shit about music. We established that."

Levon shrugged.

"How about women?" Hector said.

"My wife's been dead three years now."

"Fuck me." Hector sighed. He sat back in a puddle of his own butt sweat and wished the day to be gone.

———

The farther west they drove, the greater the military presence. The approach to Kirkuk was one roadblock stop after another. Every one of Allah's children with a gun took it into their head to set up a toll booth along Highway 80. Sometimes an armored vehicle blocked the road. Sometimes a technical; a commercial pickup with a machine gun or triple-A gun bolted down into the bed. Once it was a bunch of kids with oil drums and duct tape. They all wore bits and pieces of uniforms. They all smiled like pirates.

Hector had papers that satisfied some and they were waved on. Some were unimpressed with the documentation. Or maybe they were illiterate. An American twenty-dollar bill got them past those checkpoints.

Levon let Hector do the negotiations. Some of the kids they ran into were no older than Merry. Orphans probably. The hard set of their eyes was real enough. So were their rifles.

The only official Iraqi army checkpoint was when they came closer to Kirkuk. They wanted *forty* bucks.

The Iraqi army presence was high in Kirkuk. Uniformed soldiers and vehicles everywhere. They loitered on corners and at crossroads, showing off their weapons like kids with a new toy. And most of them *were* kids.

"Look at all these son bitches in their shiny BDUs," Hector said.

"I thought the fight was in Mosul," Levon said.

"That's why these heroes are two hundred klicks away. All the fighting is being done by your Peshmerga pals and the Iranians."

They drove past a crowd of soldiers seated in the shade of a gas station awning. Levon noted that their uniforms weren't new. They were patched and spotted with pink splotches where the blood of their previous owners had been bleached out. Their weapons were a mix of Russian and American make, and most showed signs of neglect. They probably weren't any older than the recruits he saw earlier. But they were harder.

Evidence of recent house-to-house fighting was everywhere. Bullet-scarred walls and fire-gutted buildings. Already the citizens were rebuilding. Everywhere, block-long mountains of rubble were being stacked by hand and machine. Hector pulled them to a stop on a broad boulevard crowded with pedestrians. Cars and vans honked and swerved past them.

"I'm gonna pick up some stuff at the market," he said. He nodded in the direction the majority of the crowd was walking.

"We park here, and this ride will be stripped to the chassis when we get back," Levon said.

"That's why you're going to circle the block until I get back," Hector said, stepping from the cab. He made a stirring gesture with his finger.

"Pick up a few cartons of cigarettes." Levon peeled some bills off the roll in his pocket.

"You smoke now?"

"Just buy them. American brands." Levon slid over to get behind the wheel.

"Don't even think of running off on me," Hector said. He didn't wait for a reply. He waded into the crowd and was gone.

Levon put the HiLux in gear and pulled into the moving tide of cars, trucks, and mopeds. The feel of the streets was like any other cosmopolitan city at lunch hour. Street vendors crowded the walkways with carts. The busy hustle in contrast with the sorry state of the buildings and streets. Apartment towers scorched by the bombing stood like blackened skeletons against the sky. Every other business along the street was either burned out or boarded up. Many were roofed with blue plastic tarps.

As prevalent as the blue tarps was the Kurdistan flag —a tricolor with a yellow sun. A flag for a country that didn't exist and would never exist if Syria, Iraq, Turkey, and Iran had anything to say about it. The flag hung from streetlamps and storefronts, and flew from cars and trucks. Kids wore t-shirts with it silk-screened on the front. Women wore hijabs fashioned from it. Levon noted the absence of Iraqi soldiers in the center of town. Instead, there were armed civilians everywhere. Men who looked more like they were dressed to play a few holes of golf but for the Kalashnikovs slung from their shoulders and the ammo vests belted over their polo shirts. A number of women were strapped with rifles as well—some of them in camouflaged BDUs.

The Kurds considered Kirkuk to be a Kurd city. They had been the majority of the population here before ISIS. They'd returned in even greater numbers when the city was retaken by the coalition. This whole caliphate insurrection stirred Kurdish nationalism. Even more dangerous, it put guns in their hands. Levon knew where his money was if it came to a showdown between the Kurds and the green Iraqi conscripts he saw earlier. And it would come to that.

The block was a long one, as it encircled the main city square where the market was set up. Where it had probably been set up since before the time of Christ. Hector was easy to spot on the crowded corner where Levon left him. He was taller than almost everyone and balancing a melon on one hand held over his head.

"Man, I thought you ditched me," Hector said. He piled into the passenger seat with the melon and string bags full of produce in his lap. One bag held a block of cigarette cartons. He held out a bottle of Fanta to Levon.

"It's still cold," he said.

Levon took the bottle. As he drove, he held the chilly glass to his temple.

"Got melon. Pistachios. Goat cheese. Garlic." Hector rooted through the bag.

"I smelled you before I saw you." Levon was not smiling.

"You're going to want to *smell* like the locals, right? Olfactory camouflage, am I right?"

"You're not wrong."

Levon drove them through town and toward the highway that would take them to Mosul. The sun was low in the sky, and shadows dropped down from the high face of the great citadel looming above to create a false twilight over half the city. Hector cracked pistachios and enjoyed being the passenger awhile, a boot up on the dash. Two checkpoints, one manned by kids and one official, blocked the access road back to 80. Some sodas made the kids happy. The quartet of Iraqis wanted a twenty each. Hector got them down to fifty total.

They were up on the highway and heading across a table-flat landscape turning purple as dusk approached. Ahead of them, the roadway was marked by head and tail lights of semis hauling oil tanks. Darkness closed in all around them. The string of lights moved back and forth through the black to infinity.

———

"Low on gas," Levon said. He took a hand from the wheel to punch Hector in the shoulder. The man came awake with a start. His hand moved snake-fast for the short-barrel revolver tucked in his waistband.

"We're near empty." Levon pointed to the fuel gauge on the dash.

Hector rubbed his eyes with the heels of his hands and peered forward. The high beams shone off the road before them. All else was black inkiness. They were an hour past the oil rigs of Bai Hasan and the truck traffic had died away until the highway was empty but for their HiLux. As far as Hector could tell, they were alone in the universe with only the cold light of the stars for company.

"Pull up somewhere. Up there looks level," Hector said. He pointed at a place ahead on the right.

Levon pulled to the side. The tires crunched over the broken stone. He came to a stop.

"I'm going to keep the engine running," Levon said.

"Yeah. Good idea." Hector climbed out and moved to the rear of the truck where he had jerry cans strapped down.

He unbuckled the straps and freed a five-gallon can. He snatched up a funnel with a long hose and placed it in the fuel intake. The gas glugged into the tank, the steel skin of the can making metallic pops as it emptied. He held the can in both hands to tip it up to get every drop. Hector was replacing the empty in the truck bed and reaching for the handle of a second can when he heard the grind of stones behind him.

"*Asir bekheyr,*" a voice said from the dark.

Farsi. Hector's Farsi sucked but he knew that was "good evening." The tone wished him anything but.

Two men emerged from the surrounding dark, lit in the reddish glow of the HiLux's taillights. Magnum P.I. mustaches and bad skin. They wore camo fatigues speckled gray and white. Urban camo. On their shoulders, garish red and yellow patches featured a falcon landing atop the crossbar of an anchor on a field of crossed daggers.

Iranian army.

"*Koja mikha y beri?*" the other one said.

"Sorry?" Hector said.

"English? American?" the first one said.

"Canadian," Hector lied.

The second one said something to the first one who nodded. Both raised their rifles at Hector.

"A ya taena haesti?"

Hector understood that much. *Are you by yourself?* He glanced at the truck cab. Levon Cade was nowhere in sight.

"*Baleh*," he said and never felt more alone in his life.

17

They drove through the night past dark houses of just another suburban Smurf village. Roads with names like Rambling Way and Windrift Drive curved and looped and wound back on themselves. It was a maze of identical streets lined with single homes of one and two stories on quarter-acre lots.

Merry sat upright, belted in, next to the woman from domestic services. Her name was Miss Nussbaum. Merry would have found that to be a funny name on any other day but this one.

"The Knoxes are a nice family. They already have a girl in foster. I placed her there six months ago. A couple of years older than you," Miss Nussbaum said. She tried on a smile.

Merry said nothing. She didn't want this woman to hear the catch in her voice. Her eyes still stung from crying. She held back the tears as the lump grew more and more painful in her throat. If she tried to talk, she knew that lump would come up to fill her eyes again.

"You'll be there a few weeks until we can place you somewhere more permanent. I'll be by in a few days to see how you're settling in." Miss Nussbaum glanced at the clock on the dashboard.

Merry nodded.

"I gave you my card, didn't I?"

Merry nodded again.

The car pulled to the curb at the foot of a driveway. The house was in the middle of a long block—an older split level with vinyl siding. A pair of hatchbacks sat on the cracked concrete driveway. Miss Nussbaum kept the engine running while she retrieved a bag from the back seat of her car. Some of Merry's clothes picked out for her by one of the women, a Treasury agent in big glasses, who had been at Uncle Fern's house. The petite Black woman who was very kind to Merry. She sensed that the woman's kindness wasn't pretended. Not like Miss Nussbaum or Agent Valdez.

Miss Nussbaum rang the bell. The muffled sound of a television went silent, and the door was pulled open. A woman held the door open for them. She wore cut-off jeans and slippers and a Crimson Tide T-shirt several sizes too large.

"She's white," the woman said by way of greeting. She wore a painted-on smile too.

"Well, yes," Miss Nussbaum said.

"I wasn't sure. Can't tell by names anymore," the woman said and accepted a sheaf of forms on a clipboard offered her by Miss Nussbaum. She took a pen from under the clip and began signing papers.

Merry leaned to one side to peek past the women at the room beyond. A narrow living room with wood-paneled walls. There was a sofa and two easy chairs, all covered in clear plastic. A man lay back on the sofa, watching some kind of show about fishermen on a big TV set on the far wall. The volume on mute. Merry couldn't see much but that the man was skinny and had a ponytail. He had an ashtray resting on his belly and a cigarette burned away between his fingers. A pizza box lay open on a coffee table with half a pie still left. Merry felt a gurgle in her stomach.

"This is Mrs. Knox, Merry," Miss Nussbaum said. She stooped to touch Merry's arm.

"You can call me Carrie. My husband's name is Greg." The woman nodded toward the man reclining in the next room.

"Do I have to sign a paper too?" Merry said.

The women shared a dry chuckle.

"No, that's all taken care of. You have some of your things here? I'll show you to the room you'll share with Lisa. She's another girl we're taking care of," Carrie said.

"So, we're done here?" Miss Nussbaum said. She was backing toward the doorway, anxious to leave.

"We're going to be fine. Aren't we, Merry?" Carrie smiled and tilted her head in a way she probably thought was comforting.

Merry picked up the bag while the women made their farewells. She could tell by the weight there were no books inside the bag. She didn't see any books anywhere in what little of the house she could see.

"Is there anything you need, Merry? It's late and you're probably tired," Carrie said.

Merry's stomach was tight as a fist. Her last meal was at breakfast. She would not tell this woman that. She longed to be alone, away from all adults. She wanted to be able to drop the mask she was wearing and cry to herself.

"I'll lay out your sleep clothes while you take a bath. There's fresh towels for you." Carrie took the bag from her hands and led the way up to the second floor.

Carrie showed her to the bathroom. It was a tiny room with a clawfoot tub, a sink and cracked white tile on the walls and a yellow linoleum floor. A stack of clean white towels sat on the sink counter with a new toothbrush and a bar of soap resting atop it.

"We have rules here, but they can wait until morning. I'll be taking you to the school tomorrow to get you registered. Lisa will make sure you get up on time to get dressed and have breakfast. She's the other girl we have in care. You're sharing a room." Carrie bent to put the stopper in the drain and turned on the tap in the tub.

"Will you be all right on your own?" Carrie said. She was already moving to the door.

"I'll be okay," Merry said.

"You'll find your pjs on the bed that'll be yours. Just bring your towel back to put in this hamper." Carrie pointed to a basket by the bathroom door and stepped into the hall, drawing the door closed behind her.

"Good night," Carrie said through the door.

Merry moved on tiptoe to shoot a bolt lock closed. She pulled the heavy wicker hamper across the linoleum until it was hard against the door. Then she stripped out of her clothes and added them to the laundry in the hamper. There were other rumpled articles that looked like they belonged to the other girl.

She waited until the tub was half full and stepped inside, easing down into the steaming embrace. She dipped a washcloth into the water and wrung it out to hold it against her face with both hands. Her shoulders shivered like the wings of a baby bird as she surrendered to the strangling lump in her throat. Her sobs echoed back to her off the tiles. Her tears mixed with the bathwater until the water got cold.

18

Gunny Leffertz said:

"No one holds a grudge like a Persian."

The two guys switched to Persian. One of them turned off the ignition on the HiLux and pocketed the keys. It died with a hiss and a wheeze. He tossed through the cab of the HiLux looking for swag. The other held his rifle steady on Hector. Hector didn't know much Persian. Not even enough to order a meal. He knelt on the ground with his hands clasped at the back of his head as they commented over everything they found in the truck. They stuffed the cartons of Kools and Marlboros into their tunics.

Hector's heart was pounding rabbit fast. The buzzing sound of his own rushing blood built in his ears to a deafening pulse. He raced through his options. Make a run into the dark. Make a play for one of their weapons. Every choice was bad. Doing nothing was worse.

The younger of the two Iranians poked him in the head with the barrel of an AK and asked a question.

"Yeah. I fucked your sister, motherfucker," Hector said. In English.

The Iranian didn't understand the words but caught the tone. He gave Hector a harder tap with the muzzle. It opened a scrape along Hector's scalp. Warm blood oozed through his hair to run down his neck.

They had him up and walking with kicks and prods, directing him into the greater dark. They spoke to one another at Hector's expense. They were snickering at each other's remarks. He dared himself to run into the black night. Just take off, and fuck what came next. In his mind, he was already a mile away, racing out of range of their hot rounds. His body wasn't buying the fantasy. His legs wouldn't obey.

A battered Safir, an Iranian knockoff of an American Jeep, sat on the floor of a shallow depression, down out of sight from the roadway. Trash from ration containers and empty water bottles were tossed all around. These guys had been camped here a while. They were out of the fight. Malingerers or even deserters. The vehicle had a tarp rigged from it as a makeshift tent. Two more figures sat in the gloom under the tarp, their backs to the side of the Safir. A coffee pot bubbled on a butane stove. The smell of Turkish tobacco hung in the air in a foul fug.

The older Iranian spoke to the two under the tarp. Neither man answered or moved. He kicked out at a boot. The wearer slumped sideways into the other man's lap. A thick coppery smell mingled with the odor of scorched coffee and cigarettes.

Hector threw himself to the ground and made himself as small as he could. Two barks came from the outer dark. A pair of bright white flashes. The young guy sagged to his knees, face gone. The older guy turned to meet a third round. It took him high in the chest. He tumbled against the camp stove, spilling coffee to the sand in a steaming pool.

Levon Cade stepped from the dark at a fast walk. Rifle up. He pumped a round each into the fallen men as he closed. Their bodies jerked, both stone dead, reanimated by the impacts. Hector was up on his feet in a stumble. He tripped over the tent line from the tarp, tearing it aside. Two more Iranians lay exposed, black blood from slit throats shiny in the starlight.

"Shit," Hector said. He bent to catch his breath. He disguised the motion by picking up a discarded AK.

Levon walked to the Safir and did a search of the interior. He found a Russian-made handgun and handset radio. He put the pistol in his waistband and hung the radio from his belt.

"Motherfuck," Hector said. He leaned against the fender of the Safir. He sucked air into his lungs in sips. A bellyful of dates came up to spill over one of his captors.

"Sack up. And don't forget the cigarettes," Levon said. He walked back toward the roadway.

Hector leaped up to follow. He gave his head a brisk shake.

"I thought you were combat experienced," Levon said when Hector caught up.

"House to house, point and shoot firefights. Not ninja shit like that," Hector said.

"A fight's a fight."

"You got ahead of us. Kakked those guys without a sound."

"I had to know how many of them there were."

"God damn. God damn." Hector's voice was hoarse with stomach acid. He hawked and spat.

They returned to the HiLux. Levon took charge of pouring the fuel into the tank. Hector gathered all the stuff the Iranians had pulled from the cab and put it back in place. The tank topped, Levon took the wheel, and they headed west.

Neither spoke for a few miles.

"You left me with them. How'd you know they weren't going to kill me right there?" Hector said.

"Because they were going to rape you first."

Hector turned to him. Levon's eyes were fixed on the road ahead.

"That's what they were laughing about," Hector said.

Levon nodded.

"Jesus," Hector said.

"You can thank Him too."

19

"You had to go that way?" Bill Marquez said.

"What do you mean?" Nancy Valdez said.

"The little girl. Did you have to take that angle?"

"On a major federal case? You want me to tiptoe? Baby steps?"

They were at her place in Alexandria. He offered to make dinner for them both. His specialty pasta puttanesca. All fresh ingredients he picked up at Whole Foods, along with the California red she liked. It was a silent understanding that Bill would be spending the night. A celebration of her making a major move on the case that started with him at the Bureau before her unit at Treasury took it on. A victory for both of them in a lot of ways, the investigation that brought them together in the first place.

As Bill heard more of the details from Alabama, he was feeling less celebratory.

"You're punishing the girl for what her father did?" he said. His fork was down, the meal forgotten.

"You make it sound like she was an innocent.

Meredith Cade has been with her father every step of the way on this," she said. She swirled red in her glass, her meal untouched too.

"She was an accessory? You're not serious."

"Where's any evidence to the contrary? This guy goes on a road trip over half the country leaving bodies everywhere he goes. You think she spent the whole time coloring with crayons?"

"There had to be another way."

"What way? *Tell* me. I only have this case because the FBI fucked it up and let the trail go cold. It was my team tracked this guy home while you guys were waiting for him to walk in and hand himself over. And let's look at what's going on with this guy. Multiple murders. Grand theft. Interstate flight. And the key to a fortune in stolen cash possibly. I'm talking billions potentially."

"And the little girl was in on it all. You seriously believe that?"

"Maybe she's a victim here. Maybe that's true. Her dad takes her along as an unwilling participant." Nancy shrugged. "But you haven't talked to her. She's thirteen years old with the mind of a three-time loser. Kept trying to turn the Q&A back on me. She knows more than she'll say. She knows where her father is. Maybe even where the money is."

"What's the strategy? You let foster care break her?"

"She has my card."

"Christ, Nance. That's rotten."

"And what would you do? You think she was living in some model home? A sociopath for a dad? Some old coot of an uncle living in hillbilly paradise?"

"So you're doing her favor turning her over to the system?"

"I looked for other family."

"How hard?"

Nancy slammed her glass down hard enough to slosh wine across the table.

"I thought you wanted this fucker caught." Her eyes narrowed to slits. Her head tilted, chin out.

"No one wants Cade nailed more than me. Shit, I was two steps behind him in Kansas City." Bill reached over to blot spilled wine with his napkin.

"I want him too. I need to close the books on him, justify the faith the department put in me."

"Smooth career move then." He met her eyes.

Nancy drew in a deep breath through her nose.

"You know what? Maybe you should leave."

"Yeah." He pushed back his chair and picked up his plate as he did so.

"Leave it," she said, looking away from him.

"You know I'm right," he said. He left the kitchen for the living room, picking up his suit jacket and pistol where he'd left them on the seat of an armchair.

"You know what I know?" she called after him. "You cook Italian like a Puerto Rican."

She reached for the red to top off her glass, not flinching when her door banged shut like a rifle shot. She drained the glass before taking the plates to dump them into the disposal.

20

Gunny Leffertz said:

"Soldiers come in all sizes and shapes. A kid or a woman can kill you as dead as a grown man."

The road climbed higher, and the air grew colder as they drove west. The nights were becoming damp and chilled. Soon the days would be cold, too, as winter came to Iraq.

There were more and more signs of recent combat action and troop movements as they closed on the region to the east of Mosul. Columns of refugees came their way in groups of dozens, then hundreds. There were crushed vehicles, military and commercial, lining the shoulders, the paint scorched off them. The remains of air strikes by American planes mostly. Roasted carcasses melted to the seats. Vultures lifted into lazy flight from the wreckage as they went by, only to land again after they passed. Earlier in the day, they saw an arrow formation of French Mirages boom by to the north. Miles to the west, the will of the caliphate was being tested by pinprick strikes.

More and more red pennant flags dotted the sides of the road like holiday decorations. They each marked an unexploded IED left behind by ISIS in retreat.

"This area's secured but not cleared," Hector said.

"I see them," Levon said. He kept the truck to the center of the road. He often slowed to allow refugees to cross and recross the road, giving the red flags a wide berth. Their faces were pale and drawn—the stress of living under the thumb of cruel masters enforcing an unforgiving set of laws. The threat of torture, rape, and death a daily reality. And now a flight across a godforsaken landscape to an uncertain future. Even the children looked old beyond their years.

Levon pulled the truck aside now and again to allow civilian ambulances to scream past. They were seeing more and more of the red and white vehicles marked with a crescent traveling at top speed in either direction. They were probably seeing some of the same ambulances over and over. The medical volunteers making their way from forward triage facilities to med stations farther away from the fighting.

The sounds of war reached them now. Plumes of yellow smoke bloomed along the horizon, followed seconds later by dull booms that shook the road surface under the HiLux's tires.

The first roadblock they came to was manned by Iranians, Revolutionary Guard. An armored vehicle stood by the side of the road. A helmeted gunner manned a heavy machine gun in the open turret. Soldiers nearly identical to the ones Levon had killed the night before waved them to a stop. Berets and mustaches. Uniforms in forest camo in a treeless region. Their weapons shiny with fresh oil. Their eyes hard. Levon motioned to Hector to keep his mouth shut. He exchanged words with the soldiers in Persian with a few Russian phrases thrown in. They nodded along with them and two of them reached into the cab of the HiLux to fist bump him. They waved them through, and Levon motored west.

"What's with the Russian?" Hector said.

"I told them we're Spetsnaz vets who like to fight. We came down from St. Petersburg to help take down ISIS."

"And if they asked me anything? I don't speak Russian."

"They didn't. And they didn't speak Russian either."

"You take a lot of chances, bro."

"I can let you out anytime."

"The boss told me to see you to Mosul. That's what I'm going to do," Hector said. He sat gripping his knees to keep his hands from shaking. Levon drove on as if their destination was the local Home Depot.

———

The horizon to the west was a strip of shimmering pink as the stars came out behind them. They pulled over a few times to ask directions to the Kurd encampment of the Fifth Regional Militia at Gogjali. It was near midnight and approaching the base in the dark was a dangerous prospect. They pulled the pickup into the ruins of a building to wait till morning.

When the sun rose, they found they'd chosen a Chaldean Christian church for shelter. The building was a blackened hulk with the roof partially collapsed. Every religious artifact had been defaced or shattered. What was once a fine porcelain statue of a life-sized Christ lay headless on an altar covered in dried human feces. Bas relief carvings in Aramaic that had survived millennia were scratched out by gunfire or a jackhammer. Every single crucifix was broken. The walls were covered with praise for Allah and the prophet as well as the name of the Islamic State.

In a windowless nave off the main hall of the church, Hector found a mausoleum where priests had been buried over the centuries that the church had sat here undisturbed. The tombs had been opened and the bones were strewn on the floor. Some of the graves were marked by photographs or paintings. These had been torn from their frames and trampled.

"Lot of rage here," Hector said. He rejoined Levon who was stowing their gear back in the HiLux.

"Always will be. There's a saying. 'Yemen is the birthplace of the Arab. Iraq will be his grave.'"

"Where'd you hear that one?"

"From an Arab. Check the radiator. She was running hot last night."

Hector turned the cap and dipped a finger deep into the opening. His finger came back dry but for a dirty orange stain at the tip.

"Could use a gallon," he said.

"Here. Use this first." Levon handed him a jug half full of yellow liquid.

"This is piss," Hector said after an experimental sniff.

"Yeah."

"You've been saving your piss."

"So should you. Better than wasting clean water."

"We're going to be smelling your wee," Hector said.

Hector topped off the radiator and tossed the jug aside. He wiped his hands clean in the sand and accepted a protein bar tossed to him by Levon.

"Eat it on the road," Levon said. He gunned the HiLux to life.

Off to the west, the sky was smeared with smoke from distant fuel fires. The caliphate forces burned lakes of diesel and crude oil to create an artificial cloud cover that they expected to protect them from air strikes. That wasn't discouraging any of the jet traffic they saw overhead. The cloudless yellow sky overhead was streaked with contrails that looked like lines drawn in chalk. As they flew west, some of these sprouted clouds of diamond-like chaff meant to confound anti-aircraft fire.

They came to a long earthen berm that stretched for mile after mile, running north to south. It was twenty feet at the peak, piled there by earthmovers weeks before. It was a terrestrial barrier between the ground held by the Kurds and the approach to the eastern edge of Mosul. They followed the berm north until they were met by a pair of Humvees flying Kurdish flags.

The Hummers were vehicles captured by ISIS when they took Mosul from the Iraqi army. They had been painted black by the insurgents and decorated with quotes from the prophet in swirling Arabic text, now scratched out by their new owners.

Levon pulled to a stop well shy of the pair of vehicles. He stepped from the truck with empty hands raised. He called to the gunners visible in the turrets. Hector stepped clear on the opposite side, hands visible and smile fixed.

One of the gunners called back and walked toward the waiting trucks. Hector followed.

Peshmerga in matching camo BDUs climbed out of both vehicles to walk forward. All were cleanly shaven, as was common among the Kurds to separate them from their enemies. They held their weapons low but trained toward the strangers. Levon kept talking and smiling. The lead soldier called back. Hector was surprised to hear a woman's voice. As they closed the distance, he could see that they were all young women. Some looked like teenagers. Dark hair worn pinned under their caps or cropped short. They had the long thin noses of Kurdish girls. Their eyes were dark as a moonless night except for the officer who had eyes of a startling pale gray.

Levon spoke to them in a language Hector couldn't follow. Their ready stances relaxed. The gray-eyed officer brushed a stray lock of hair from her eyes and nodded along. She then pointed away up the berm in a stream of words Hector assumed were directions. Levon said something in reply, and the officer gifted them with a smile that turned her from Xena, warrior princess to the girl next door in an instant. They returned to their vehicles and drove away in a fog of yellow dust.

"You're a player, dog. You speak Kurd too?" Hector said.

"Mostly southern Kurdish. My Kurmanji isn't at an expert level, but she understood me enough to give us directions."

"They know where your friend is?"

"They didn't know Bazît. But there's a Yazidi unit five klicks up along the berm. They said he'd probably be there. They told us to keep to this side of the berm. Daesh is everywhere on the other side."

Levon turned to walk back to the HiLux. Away to the south, a pair of Apache choppers moved like wasps, noses down and gunshot. Somewhere beyond their line of sight, someone was catching hell. The chain guns made a steady purring sound. Black 20mm shell casings tumbled through the air in their wake. It was another reminder of how close they were to the fighting.

"That little officer was cute, wasn't she?" Hector said when they reached the truck.

"I didn't notice." Levon slid behind the wheel.

"Bullshit. How could you not?"

"I didn't. And I suggest you don't either."

"Doesn't hurt to look, bro."

"Out here it does. They'll have your balls off." Levon shoved the HiLux in gear and pointed them north along the foot of the berm.

21

A strange girl touched her shoulder to rock her gently.

"Your name's Merry?"

"What?" Merry said, rolling onto her back.

"I'm Lisa, and you need to get up."

A girl maybe two or three years older than her looked down at Merry. Dirty blonde hair, uncombed. A long, graceful neck atop narrow shoulders, bare under a too-large tank top. A pretty girl but for a pair of sad eyes that regarded Merry wearily.

"If you don't get up, you don't eat. House rules."

Hunger overcame whatever mix of emotions Merry might be feeling. She dressed in jeans and a Marines T-shirt and was down the stairs right after Lisa left the room. She let her nose lead her to the back of the house where bacon was frying.

The Knox family sat at a Formica table in the kitchen. Carrie and the man with the ponytail who was watching TV the night before. Greg. And a boy, maybe seventeen, rangy with close-cropped hair but for a bushy patch at the crown of his head. They each had plates and glasses and cups before them. Lisa was at the range scooping from a pan of scrambled eggs.

"Take a plate, honey," Carrie said. She nodded at a place set for Merry next to Mr. Knox, who gifted her with a grunt. The boy looked up, gave Merry an up-and-down glance. He returned his attention to the smartphone in one hand, while shoveling cold cereal with the other.

Merry scraped the last of the eggs from the pan and forked up the remaining three strips of bacon. She added two slices of toast to the plate and turned to sit down. Lisa stood at the sink scooping food to her mouth.

"Lisa. How many times I have to tell you to sit down when you eat?" Carrie said.

"M'okay here, Carrie. Almost done anyway."

"I don't give a shit. You're getting crumbs on the tile, and who's gonna clean that up?"

"I'll wipe it up," Lisa said. She forked the last into her mouth.

"Sit," Carrie said. It was a command. The one word was filled with menace.

Lisa said nothing more and slid onto the chair next to the boy. He gave her a look, a very different look than the one he'd given Merry. Lisa sat rigidly, not moving to return his gaze. Her eyes looked forward, not focused on anything. The boy sniffed and went back to tabbing his phone.

Merry cleaned her plate and poured a glass of milk.

"You can get yourself to school this morning?" Carrie said. This was to Lisa.

"I can drive her," the boy said.

"I'll walk," Lisa said. She pushed herself from the table.

"Better start now then," Carrie said. "I'm running late, and I have to take the new one to the middle school to register."

Lisa was gone from the room; her boots stomped on the steps to the second floor.

"And you brush your teeth, and wash your face," Carrie said, turning to Merry.

"Yes, Carrie." Merry drained her glass and got up to leave the table.

"And this is Blaine, my son," Carrie said. "This is Merry, Blaine."

"Hey," Blaine said without raising his eyes from texting.

"Hello," Merry said.

She left the room for the stairs. Carrie called after her that they would meet out at the car. She stood against the banister to allow for Lisa rushing down. The older girl was gone, the screen door banging, a book bag over her shoulder. Merry climbed the stairs in a hurry for their shared room.

The new one. That's all she was now. The latest in a line of strange children to be parked here in this house of strangers until they found her another house of strangers to live with.

No tears now. The well was dry. She'd keep on until she found another way. She'd do whatever she needed to do to make it through this time as an unwelcome guest in a hard world. She'd fight to be the same Merry Cade as she'd always been until her daddy came home and set the world right again.

22

Gunny Leffertz said:

"Soldiers come in all sizes and shapes. A kid or a woman can kill you as dead as a grown man."

Uniformed men lay at intervals on the western flank at the peak of the long berm. They were dug into embrasures, covered over with tarps for shade and concealment. Gun barrels pointed east to cover the empty ground of the de facto border between Kurdistan and the caliphate.

As Levon and Hector drove north, they could hear the sporadic boom of big bore rifles coming from the ridge above. Staccato pops echoed faintly from the other side, fading away whenever Apaches or Cobras wheeled into view above.

"I thought those fuckers were in retreat," Hector said. He squinted up to see a man silhouetted against the skyline give the finger to an enemy invisible on the other side of the berm.

"Nothing more dangerous than an enemy in retreat. You read much history?" Levon said.

"I watch all that Nazi shit on the history channel."

"Then you know the Germans were as good at withdrawing as they were at attacking. Same with Napoleon, Mao, Washington, Robert E. Lee, and the ancient Greeks."

"You read a lot of that stuff."

"Had to. My old gunny made me hit the books. Told me that every combat situation that could happen had already happened."

"You had a Marine sergeant made you read?"

"Gunny wasn't just an NCO. He was practically my dad."

"Shit, Cade," Hector said with a whoop. "We finally found something to talk about."

"What?" Levon said.

"You. Your story."

Levon turned from the wheel to meet Hector with dead eyes.

"Or not." Hector shrugged.

———

They pulled to a stop to join the end of a line of refugees queued up before a gate set in a lower berm that ran perpendicular to the taller border earthworks. The ragged column of civilians stretched almost a quarter mile. Each man and woman was burdened with everything from cloth sacks to Louis Vuitton luggage. Their every possession held in their hands or slung from their backs. The sound of gunfire *pop-pop-popped* from the other side of the berm. No one looked toward the source. No one flinched. They'd lived month after month with the noise of war as a soundtrack to their lives. It was as common a noise as the wind.

The crowd was weary, but a lot of smiles could be seen. Children teased and laughed like children everywhere. And they were scolded back into line as parents everywhere will do. This sad collection of humanity was finally away from the constant threat of betrayal, abuse, and death. The mood was of travelers finally at the end of an arduous journey not of their choosing. They did not know what was ahead. They only knew that they wanted no more of what they left behind.

Enormous Yazidi flags flew above a pair of towers constructed of stacked HESCO barriers that flanked either side of the opening. A red bar atop a white bar. Inside the red field was a yellow sun. Within the yellow sun, a symbol of the unusual god that Yazidis worshipped: a peacock king.

Atop the towers, soldiers leaned on mounted .50 caliber machine guns to cover the approaching crowd. The path to the opening was blocked by oil barrels loaded with dirt and rocks to constrict passage to two or three people at a time. The way wasn't wide enough to allow passage of vehicles. More rock-filled HESCOs dotted the approach in a staggered pattern to prevent vehicles from coming near the checkpoint.

"This is where we get out." Levon climbed from the cab.

"Remember where we parked," Hector said.

He pocketed the keys and followed Levon around to the bed of the truck. Levon distributed water out of their remaining water jugs to some of the people awaiting entry into the Yazidi zone. There were Kurds, Arabs, and Iraqis mixed in the group.

The flight from the caliphate erased all tribal differences. For now.

Hector dropped the tailgate to slide his arms into the straps of a backpack.

"You sure we'll be welcome, brother?" Hector said. He slipped the combat sling of his rifle to hang from his shoulder.

"Bazît's a kind of folk hero to these people. All we need to do is find him."

"If he's still alive."

"He's a hard man to kill."

Levon poured water into cups and mugs held out to him by women anxious for water for their thirsty children. Hector heard him offering words of comfort to the mothers and even saw the man smiling. They ducked their heads in thanks, smiling and giving thanks. Hector stepped up onto the tailgate to dig into a sack of MREs. Joining the party, Levon started to wing them over the heads of the crowd. Men snagged them out of the air while Hector called colorful commentary.

"That's an easy out! Good catch there, Sammy! Look at this guy! Magic hands!"

Levon moved along the line offering water from the jugs held under his arms. He moved through the crush to approach a young woman in a khimar shawl. She carried a baby bundled in her arms. She turned from him, fear plain in her eyes.

"For your baby," he said in Farsi, then in Kurd.

She lowered her head and moved along the line away from him into a clutch of men waiting along the edge of the crowd. Holding the jugs over his head, Levon waded after her. The women pressed closer, imploring him to share the water. He handed the jugs off to hands outstretched toward him and shoved his way toward the young woman and baby.

The woman saw him and broke into a run. She raced, head down, for the place where the line became constricted to enter the HESCO barrier maze. People waiting for entry crowded there in a dense pack. Levon held his M4 over his head to squeeze out three rounds. The crowd around him collapsed to the ground. Up at the checkpoint, voices shouted back and forth. The loud metallic clack of bolts drawn back on the Ma Deuces up atop the towers. Levon shrugged off his pack and sprinted forward after the young woman. She stumbled as a sandal flew from one foot. She clutched the bundle closer to her to run headlong into the packed queue of refugees crouched in the chokepoint. Levon slammed into her back, driving her hard against a wall of HESCOs.

The world went white in that instant then deepest black.

23

Most of the morning of her first day of school was spent in the school office. A picture was taken for her student ID card. A form to sign giving the school permission to retrieve her school records from Huntsville. Questions about her medical history. And about her two-year absence from school. She was assigned a locker. The rest of the morning was spent waiting on benches outside offices until they had a neat little file made up on her and a class schedule worked out.

It was decided that she be set back a year, making her the tallest girl in her class. She didn't think this was fair. They didn't even test her.

It was near the end of the third period by the time Merry was sent to a classroom. The lesson was almost over when she entered the room. She handed a note to the teacher who pointed out an empty chair near the back of the room. The class was Environmental Science. The teacher read in a droning voice from a notebook open on his desk. Most of the kids ignored him to play with their phones. Games and texting. One kid, a few seats up in the next row, looked like he was taking notes. Merry craned to see the page of his notebook. He was absorbed in drawing a picture of a superhero fighting a robot.

For the rest of the day, except by her teachers, Merry was largely ignored. The other kids disregarded her, absorbed in their own friendships and cliques. Otherwise, it was just another day at Calhoun Middle School.

School seemed so boring now. Or maybe it was always boring, and she never noticed before, distracted by her own friends and cliques. Her routine had been broken when she went on the run with her father. There had been no regimentation to her life. Every day was different with her daddy. Back in school again, everything was routine and rote. Roll calls, assigned seats, changing classes, and every moment of the day scheduled to the minute.

Lunch came around and she was starved. Mrs. Knox had not given her money for lunch or packed anything for her. Sitting in the cafeteria watching the other kids eat was torture. She walked out onto an asphalt courtyard in the elbow of the long L-shaped building. She could still hear the rise and fall of the buzzing conversation from the cafeteria. But she was alone and enjoying the solitude.

She walked around outside, hugging her arms to her. It was a warm day for the time of year, but still she was chilled. There was no coat for her at the house. Out in the school back lot, there was a pair of basketball stanchions, the chain nets tinkling in the breeze. Some concrete benches and sickly evergreen trees. Beyond them was a prefab building set up on blocks, with wooden steps and a broad deck leading to a double doorway. Above the doors was a sign informing her that this was the school library.

Inside was warm and dry. The white noise of the central heating unit on the roof closed out the sounds from outside. There were long, empty tables with chairs pulled in. Rows of steel shelves were lined with books of all sizes with colorful spines. The smell of old paper and glue everywhere. And another scent that made Merry's mouth water. Cooked onions and something sweet. She stepped around a row of spin racks, pockets sagging with old magazines, to find a long counter of blond wood.

"Oh," the woman behind the counter said. A petite woman in a Calhoun sweatshirt. She looked bird-like, with angled glasses set atop a long nose. Her black hair, fringed with gray above the ears, was pulled back into an untidy braid. A pair of pencils poked from the bundle.

"I'm sorry," Merry said. She backed away.

"Are you with a class?" the woman said.

"No. Just me."

"Where's your class?"

"At lunch."

"Hungry for knowledge instead of PB and J?" The woman smiled at her own joke, encouraging Merry to share it. It was an open smile that made her eyes crinkle.

"Both, I guess," Merry said. She returned the smile.

"Well, as usual, I brought too much from home." The woman held up a pair of chopsticks, a pea pod expertly grasped between them.

"I don't want to bother anyone," Merry said. She took another step back, her eyes fixed with longing on the shiny green wedge.

"Don't be silly. I'll wind up throwing half of this out

anyhow." The woman gestured for Merry to join her behind the counter.

Merry had never had Chinese food before and certainly had never eaten with anything other than a fork and spoon. Ms. Booth, that was her name, showed Merry how to position the sticks between her fingers and thumb. After a few near misses, and one disc of water chestnut sent flying into the book returns, she got the hang of it. She dug into a delicious mix of rice, chicken, and some veggies that she was tasting for the first time in her life.

As grateful as she was for lunch, she enjoyed the conversation even more. Ms. Booth insisted that Merry call her 'Coco.' This forced a giggle from Merry. She sprayed rice onto the carpet. The giggle only deepened as Ms. Booth insisted that Coco was indeed the name her parents had given her.

"People always think I'm kidding them," Coco said.

"I'm sorry I laughed," Merry said.

"It's okay. I grew up with all the jokes. 'Coo-coo for Coco Puffs!'"

Merry snorted.

Coco didn't ask her any questions beyond school and books and things like that. Merry only told her that she was new, and this was her first day. She told herself that the story of how she wound up in foster care was too complicated to share. What she really felt was a shame she couldn't understand. This was the worst time in her short life so far, worse even than losing her mother to cancer. Worse even than the peculiar and uncertain life she lived with her father. At least, in the middle of all the chaos, her father was a constant. And now all constancy was gone and somehow, she felt it might be her fault.

But Merry was happy to forget all of that for the moment. The library was always her favorite place at school, and today it was a refuge.

It was the librarian's turn to laugh when Merry told her that Mickey Spillane was her favorite writer. Merry told her about her uncle's vast library of paperback mysteries and Marine Corps histories.

"Not exactly Harry Potter," Coco said.

"That magic stuff's okay but I like the private eye stuff more," Merry said.

"Nothing wrong with Mike Hammer. You might like Raymond Chandler too."

"Who's that? Do you have any here?"

"Sadly, no. A little above the required public school reading list for junior high. But I have some at home I'd be glad to let you borrow."

"That would be great. I think I heard the bell. I'd better get back. Thank you for lunch, Coco," Merry said, beaming. She set down her bowl and slid from the stool.

"Well, thank you for the company. It's not every day a student comes into the library of their own free will," Coco said, returning Merry's farewell wave.

24

Gunny Leffertz said:

"If you're hurtin', you're alive."

He could hear but not see.

There were voices speaking somewhere. The ambient sounds of a room, wind rustling through shifting cloth. The clink of a glass. Someone coughing. Far away the thump of a generator.

The smell of rubbing alcohol and something else, something corrupt, beneath it.

He opened his lids to gray darkness.

There was pressure across the bridge of his nose. His face was wrapped in cloth from his upper lip to above his brow. He made to touch the bandages. His elbows would not bend. Restraints.

A gentle hand touched his shoulder and told him to

relax, to place his fate in God's hands. The voice was feminine. The language was English with the trace of an accent.

"My eyes," he said. His voice an arid croak.

"They are intact. Your sight is not damaged."

The woman's fingertips remained on his shoulder while she turned to speak to someone, a man—an exchange in Kurdish.

"You will sleep now," she said when she turned back to him.

He made to respond but his mouth filled with cotton. The gray field before his eyes turned to speckles of yellow. A warm tide washed over him until his head was submerged and he was gone from all care.

———

"Wake up, you crazy fucker."

Levon came around to find himself in a double row of bunks in a long tent structure. Men in various stages of consciousness filled the ward. More were lying on the ground between bunks. Hector Ortiz was standing at the foot of his bunk.

"You're lucky to be alive," Hector said. He was grinning, but his eyes looked tired.

"Am I?"

"Lucky?"

"Alive."

"Well, you managed to fuck yourself up. But, yeah, you're a lucky one. That bitch only managed to set off her detonator. The full charge didn't blow."

The restraints were off Levon's arms. He could touch

his face. One side of his head was shaved, and there were fresh sutures around one ear and over one eye. His eyes burned and felt gritty. The vision was blurred—more in the left eye than the right. His torso was wrapped tight in stretch gauze.

"The haji chick took most of the blast. You broke some ribs and nearly lost that ear."

"My eyes."

"Chemical burns. No permanent scarring, they tell me. Some Aussie missionary doctors patched you up. One of them is hot."

The accented voice. The gentle fingertips.

With an effort Levon sat up and swung his bare feet to the floor.

"Hold on there, brother. You're in no shape to deploy," Hector said. He reached out to press Levon back onto the bunk. Levon shoved him away.

"I won't get better laying here," he said. He levered up, using his arms, standing, shaky at first.

Hector looked down at the man lying on the floor between Levon's and the next bunk. The guy had blood-caked tubes running under stained bandages. His eyes and mouth were wide open. Hector watched an ant crawl over the guy's tongue and out onto his chin.

"Sure. Sure. Let's get your ass out of here," Hector said. He made to give Levon a supporting hand. His reward was to have his fingers brushed away. Levon found his BDUs, stiff with dried blood, and slid them on. There was no shirt and no shoes. His gear was gone.

A nurse half his size attempted to stop him. He waved her away. Hector shook his head at her. They made their way through the maze of bunks and makeshift nurse stations to the cold night outside. The medical tent was in a long row of similar structures along with some battered ready-made Conex huts. There were flat-roofed buildings beyond them, backlit by green halogen lights along a fenced perimeter.

The place was on a war footing hustle. Vehicles of all kinds carried wounded to the med compound. Armed men were everywhere. Most were young men in uniform. Clean shaven but for a few older men wearing the brushy mustache favored by married Yazidi men. Others were civilian militia, including women. A gaggle of children chased a goat among the wicket of guy wires strung from the tents. The goat nimbly jumped the lines as the children tripped and clambered, giggling, behind it.

"Is Bazît here in camp?" Levon said.

"Yeah. He heard about some crazy white guy jumping a suicide bomber and came to check you out," Hector said.

"So, he is alive."

"Yeah. And he thinks you're the shit, Cade. Also thinks you're as crazy as I do. They told me some stories that have to be half bullshit."

The rich smell of cooked meat came between the tents. Levon's stomach clenched tight as a fist.

"I need to eat," he said.

"My treat," Hector said. They followed the greasy scent of lamb and onions.

———

They were welcomed to share in a pair of sheep roasting on spits over an open fire. There were piles of unleavened bread and some kind of mashed squash. Strong coffee with sweet goat cream. Levon and Hector took a seat on the ground with some of the men.

Some kids were gathered around the electric glow of a television watching cartoons. A line of women in camo BDUs danced shoulder to shoulder in a rhythm to some Sufi dirge playing on a battered boombox set atop an oil drum. A slow, desultory step with heads lowered and faces dour. A dance of mourning.

The men about the fire nodded to them and made gestures of greeting. There were no smiles but there was respect. Someone found Levon a uniform tunic in forest camo. He wore it draped over his shoulders.

One of the men, a few years older than Levon, shared pictures with them on his mobile phone. A son about twenty. Three daughters ranging from pre-adolescent to teen. Pictures from a family wedding. From dinners and from schoolhouses. Levon exchanged words with the man in Kurmanji. The firelight gleamed off tears in the man's eyes. They looked out of place on his hard features.

"What's the story?" Hector said. He waggled fingers at the bright images on the mobile screen.

"He's from Sinjar. Islamic State came in the middle of the night. They killed the men. His son. Took his wife and daughters." Levon handed the phone back to the man with a few words of sympathy.

"Where was he?"

"Away helping a cousin who was ill. He says he wishes he had been there, died there. He would have used any weapon to kill the Daesh. He will die killing as many of them as he can."

"Jesus."

"He says that he knows what has happened to his daughters, but he will forgive them. He will welcome them back. The Yazidi faith used to be as unforgiving about rape as the Koran. But since all this happened, the Yazidi sheiks have prayed to the angels and voted to change their religious laws."

"Nice of them," Hector said. He made a *pfft* sound with his lips.

"That's a big accommodation for them. Any woman who escapes or is bought back from Daesh makes a pilgrimage to Lalish. That's their sacred village. She can be cleansed there. Made whole."

"Does this guy know where his family is?"

"They could be anywhere. ISIS is selling off women to men all over in an open sex market. Syria. Egypt. Saudi Arabia. Or they could have been forced into marriage with a Daesh fighter."

"Fuckers."

"And Yazidi women get a high price."

"Some of them have light hair. I even saw some blondes with green eyes. What's the deal?" Hector glanced toward the line of dancing women. There were a few in the line, their hair sun-streaked and with long curls, that would have fit right in at a Kenny Chesney concert.

"Nobody's really sure where Yazidis are from originally. According to their faith they've always been here, direct from the seed of Adam after the fall of Eden," Levon said.

"So, they're Christians?"

"No. They believe in the same god of the Bible. But

they also believe that God left the earth in trust to seven immortal beings to rule. They're something like angels."

"Seven Spanish angels in the valley of the gun."

"You told me you don't like country music."

"Don't. My dad's a Willie Nelson fan. You two could hang. What's the picture of the bird I see everywhere?"

"That's the Peacock Angel, the head being who watches over mankind."

"I never even heard of Yazidis until a week ago."

"There's less than a million of them in the world," Levon said.

"And less than that now," Hector said.

A trio of uniformed men crossed the open space around the fire on a direct line for Levon. They had weapons combat slung across their chests. Their faces were flickering masks of menace in the flame glow. Hector started to rise. Levon pressed a hand to his knee to keep him seated.

The shortest of the men stood over Levon, fixing him with a scowl. The guy looked like a pirate with a raised scar of puckered white flesh running down his face to his throat on one side. Close-cropped hair, black with flecks of white. A badass biker's goatee.

"I thought I told you never to come back here, you son of a bitch," the pirate said through clenched teeth in heavily accented English.

"And I thought I told you the best part of you ran down your mama's leg," Levon said. Both men froze, eyes locked on one another.

Hector was startled by an explosion of laughter from the smaller man. The pirate grabbed Levon's arm and yanked the bigger man to his feet and into waiting arms.

Levon let out a grunt as his ribs were pressed tight. Manly hugs and bear paw back pats.

"Ortiz, meet Bazît Hassan," Levon said when they broke their embrace.

Pounding Sufi drums kicked in on the boombox, and the girls picked up the pace of their dance as men whooped and fired rifles into the sky.

25

Merry found Lisa waiting in front of the Circle K. It was midway between Calhoun Middle and the high school. Lisa was with some other girls her age. They were standing on the walk at the side of the convenience store, smoking cigarettes. Obeying adolescent protocol, Merry did not join them. She took a seat on a steel bench at the front of the store and watched a young Black couple discuss movie picks in front of a Redbox.

The Knox hatchback pulled up and honked. Lisa ditched her cigarette and raced to take the shotgun seat. The bay door slid open to allow Merry into the back.

"Where's Blaine?" Mrs. Knox said from behind the wheel.

Lisa shrugged.

"I didn't see him," Merry said.

"Shit," Mrs. Knox said. She pulled into an open slot in front of the store and they waited until Blaine showed up, five minutes later. He winced at having to sit in the back, but said nothing beyond a grunt. Merry scooted against the opposite window to allow him room to sprawl. He spent the ride home watching the back of Lisa's head with curious interest. She sat looking forward, eyes on the road as if she were the one driving. Merry sensed something between them. In the end, she decided it was teenage stuff and turned her attention to the homes and businesses going by.

———

There was nothing to do.

She regretted not bringing home something to read. As she was given no homework assignments, Merry left her textbooks in the locker at school. Even though they were boring, she wished that she'd brought one of them home, just to have something to read.

Carrie Knox made the house rules clear on the drive home. Merry would be expected to keep tidy her half of the room she shared with Lisa, including making her own bed each morning. She would also empty the dishwasher and fold towels. She was not allowed to use the phone, and the television was off-limits except for two hours on the weekends. The rest of her time was hers to do with what she wished.

Merry thought that even a few more chores would at least pass the time. She thought about asking Carrie if she could help with dinner. Carrie was working in the kitchen, a phone held in the crook of her shoulder. Her voice was raised to compete with the noise from the television in the living room where Blaine had a sports channel turned to high volume. It sounded like she was complaining to a person on the other end. How hard she worked. How no one appreciated it. How she'd like to just get in the car and drive far, far away.

Rather than interrupt, Merry went outside to the quiet of the fenced-in backyard. There were few amusements to be had out there. A swing set sagged on a patch of sand. Probably Blaine's when he was little. It was crusted with rust. There was a tennis ball lying in the grass. She picked it up, but it was flat.

A yip from the other yard made her look up. A dog was braced against the chain link fence that separated the Knox yard from the neighbor's. A big yellow Lab smiled a dopey smile at her. She smiled back and pitched the flat tennis ball over the fence. The dog whirled to chase it and returned to the fence with the ball clamped in its teeth, tail wagging.

Merry plucked the ball from the dog's mouth and threw it again. The dog bounded away and returned. This time she gave it a scratch behind the ears. The Lab leaned its head on her arm, panting. She threw the ball a few more times before the back door of the house opened and a woman in a bathrobe called the dog in. Merry waved at the woman, who simply glared for a few seconds before turning away, the screen door banging behind her.

"Hey."

It was Blaine at the back door of the Knox house. He held the door open with a put-upon expression meant to tell the world that he was just not into any of this in any way.

"Tell my dad dinner's ready," he said.

"Where is he?" Merry said.

"The garage." The door slammed closed.

Merry opened a gate that let her out onto a driveway that ended at a cinder block garage building. The door was open. Machine sounds came from inside.

"Cool," Merry said at the sight of an old-looking two-seater car up on blocks. The hood was off, and the engine compartment was empty. The engine sat on a metal stand at the back of the garage. Greg was at a workbench operating a drill press. Merry waited until the shrill whine of the drill died down.

While she waited, she looked at the walls. Among the tools hanging from pegboard panels were pictures of helicopters and jets.

"Excuse me. Mr. Knox?" she said when the drill stopped.

Greg turned, startled.

"Who told you you could come in here?" His words were sharp.

"Mrs. Knox says dinner is ready."

"I'll be in." He turned back to the piece on the drill plate, scraping at it with a rat-tail file.

"You like airplanes and stuff?" Merry stepped closer to look at a framed photo of a helicopter bristling with weapons soaring over treetops.

"I was an engineer at Boeing down in Huntsville."

"You don't do that anymore?"

"I'm retired on disability." He sighed and turned his back to clamp the metal piece into a vise mounted on his workbench.

Greg didn't look disabled to Merry in any way except that he seemed lazy. She looked into the car, an open-top convertible. The leather seats had a vinyl cover over them. Strands of wires hung from ports in the dash. Bits and pieces of the car were everywhere. The spoked wheels hung from a beam in the ceiling.

"I helped my daddy rebuild a car," she said.

"I'm sure you did." Greg sniffed.

"For real. A '67 Mustang. It was all torn apart like this one."

"A Mustang. I guess your father considered that a classic." His voice had a bitter tinge.

"It turned out beautiful," she said.

He set the rasp down with a clank and turned to her.

"Look, I really don't give a shit. You kids are Carrie's thing. Stop bothering me and run on back and tell her I'll be along." A cigarette bobbed between yellow teeth as he spoke.

Merry backed from the garage and walked back down the drive. She could see the tree-lined street at the end of the drive. A feeling floated in her belly that made her lightheaded. What if she didn't go back into the yard, into the house? What if she just kept walking out onto the street? Turned right or left and kept going until she was blocks, *miles*, away. Go on the run like she did with her daddy.

Only that took money, and she had none.

She was surprised to find herself almost to the front walk. She looked up and down the street. A gust of wind stirred leaves along the gutter. Merry turned back and went into the house. It felt like a walk of miles.

26

"Have they asked for a ransom for your girls?" Levon said.

"They have not. It does not matter. I have no money. No way to pay," Bazît said.

"Your wife?"

"I only heard that she is dead."

They walked together between the long rows of refugee tents. The tents were dark. Lanterns off so as to not draw fire from the snipers who crept nightly over the top of the border berm. Radios played softly, music or voices. The neat rows of tents ended at the lip of a broad depression that held the community corral of sheep and goats, closed in by a circle of wire fence and steel posts. The two men stopped at the fence line, eyes on the current of woolen backs shifting under the silver moon.

"You came a long way for nothing, my friend," Bazît said.

"I made you a promise."

"I did not ask you to. Why should you keep a promise that your country has never kept?"

"It wasn't my country making the promise. It was me. An oath I took. To you."

"It is a useless gesture. My girls are gone, and no one has offered to take ransom from me."

"It's possible though. Daesh can be paid to release hostages," Levon said.

"It happens sometimes. They text or email using contact information from those they've taken." Bazît crouched. Elbows on knees, fingers steepled before him.

"Has anyone you know been contacted?"

"Oh yes. A few."

"Any who were in Baiji?"

"What is your idea, my friend?"

"We have no intel. We have no idea where your girls are. Maybe someone taken at the same time could give us a location on them. At least get us close."

"There is Farhad Aman. He was my supervisor at the oil collection station."

"An executive? Daesh contacted him about who?"

"His wife and two young sons. Taken the same time as my Kani and Rona. The dogs reached him on his phone. They let his wife speak to him. They asked for a million euros or like worth in dollars. Pounds."

"He can't pay?"

"Farhad is paid more than me but is not wealthy. Daesh thought the oil company would pay the price. Not the Chinese. They will never pay unless it is one of their own. They fired him from his job. What is one Kurd more or less to them?" Bazît spat.

"Where's Farhad now?" Levon took a knee by him.

"Kirkuk the last time I saw him."

"You could contact him?"

"I could. But of what use is it, Levon?"

"Get ahold of him. Call him. I'll talk to him."

"He has no money," Bazît said.

"Money's the one problem I don't have," Levon said.

27

With Carrie's permission, Merry made a cheese and pickle sandwich for her lunch the next morning. She added an apple and a napkin to a plastic Target shopping bag. She also found a flannel lined denim jacket in a downstairs closet. It hung on her like a sack and smelled vaguely of someone else's sweat, but it was warm.

She spent the morning thinking of nothing but lunch. Not about the sandwich and apple, but her visit to the library.

"You brought your own today," Coco said. "Good thing. Mine is cottage cheese and orange wedges today."

Merry made a face.

"Yeah. Pretty bleak." Coco shrugged.

"Did you remember those books?" Merry said.

"I did!" Coco rooted in a big canvas bag and came up with a pile of three well-loved paperbacks. *The Big Sleep*; *Farewell, My Lovely*; and *The High Window*.

"Do I read them in order?"

"Doesn't really matter."

"How long can I keep them?

"Until you're done with them. Trust me, I have plenty to read." Coco's swept an arm to take in the shelves of books around her.

"Do you have a bag or something I can put them in? I don't want them to get messed up."

"You don't have a bookbag?"

Merry shook her head. Coco stepped around a wall behind the counter and came back with a green canvas bag with an American flag patch sewn on the flap.

"All yours, thanks to the lost and found," Coco said.

"But doesn't it belong to someone else?" Merry said. She took the bag in her hands. It was worn but clean. The flag was faded by the sun and years of washings.

"Been here for years. The kid's probably in college by now."

Merry stowed the paperbacks in the bag. She was just finishing her apple when the bell rang, ending lunch period.

"Hope you like the books," Coco said by way of farewell as Merry raced for the schoolyard.

"I *know* I will!" she called back and burst out into the sunshine.

28

The fat man was a person of many names.

To Iraqis, he was Baravan Masri. To Kurds, he was Birousk Massa. To the French, he was Barteux Macca. To the English and Americans, Barry Marx. He was whatever his customers wished him to be. Muslim, Jew, Chaldean, Sunni, Shi'ite. He was what he needed to be. It was all the same god, was it not? All men lived under the same sun and moon.

Known to all, friend to none. Though no one liked him, they trusted his word.

Baravan Masri sold women.

His customers were husbands, fathers, and sons who wanted their wives, daughters, mothers, and sisters returned to them. He dealt in human flesh, and his clients were aggrieved Iraqis, Syrians, Kurds, and Yazidis seeking the return of loved ones from the sex slavery of Daesh. His partners were the emirs of ISIS, who sought cash rewards in exchange for surrendering captive women and children back to their families.

The money paid, funds in the millions since the

Islamic State swept over Syria and Iraq two years earlier, was never called ransom by Baravan. He referred to the funds as exchange fees, from which he took a small percentage. The size of that percentage was never revealed. But the size of the gems on the rings that encircled his fingers told a story of their own.

Baravan's business was quasi-legal, organized as a non-profit charity in the murky shadow world of non-governmental agencies. That he took a generous salary for his work was little compensation for the dirty work he performed at great personal risk to his ever-spreading hide. That was the way *he* saw it, in any case.

To the naïve, he was a caring individual who facilitated the freedom of women cruelly captured by dangerous fanatics. Those with both eyes open saw him as he was. A facilitator without heart or soul or any interest beyond profit. Lower than a thief. Worse than a pimp. He traded in misery.

The fat man was smiling through a sheen of sweat as he crossed the lobby to the desk of the bank manager. The dry, chill air within the International Bank of Lebanon off Pirman Street in Erbil enveloped him. The fat on the back of his neck shivered like gelatin. Perspiration turned to beads of ice water on his back. He wriggled as the drops rolled into the waistband of his silk underwear.

The manager stood to greet him. It was a greeting as cold as the air inside the bank.

"Mr. Masri, may I have a glass of water brought for you?" the manager said with a curt bow. He motioned the fat man into the guest chair set beside his desk.

"With a wedge of lemon, *sil vous plait*?" the fat man said as he dropped into the chair. A worn leather case rested across his knees. A silver chain secured the handle to a cuff on his wrist.

"Would an orange slice do?" The manager nodded to a young man seated on a stool against a column. He snapped his fingers and pointed to a carafe of water set on a cart against a wall.

"If it is all you have," the fat man said, displeased and making no effort to conceal it behind a fixed smile.

The bank manager opened a laptop and tapped a few keys while they waited for the boy to bring the ice water. Baravan Masri made a show of examining his fingernails. The boy brought the water, setting the sweating glass atop a paper coaster on the marble desktop. He retreated with a nodding bow. The fat man took a long, noisy sip.

"Your accounts have updated as of this morning. A half million euros deposited in the account for the World Rescue Initiative." The manager's mouth curled around the words. The funds came from an unidentified bank in Panama.

"Mm. Hmm." Baravan nodded, the glass to his thick lips as he sipped.

"I suppose you know what the funds are earmarked for."

The fat man unbuckled the straps of the leather case and reached within to withdraw a leather notebook. He removed a thick rubber band that held it closed. He thumbed through the pages until finding the one he wanted.

"Would you be so kind as to read me the SWIFT transfer number?" Baravan said. He touched the cool surface of the water glass to his sweating forehead.

The manager read from the screen while Baravan,

lips moving, checked the long string of numbers and letters against the one penciled in his book.

"All is in order. I will need to transfer half of that amount to the following account." Baravan said. He read a long sequence of numbers and letters from his notebook. The bank manager copied them down on a sheet of paper and read them back. He recognized the prefix code of a bank in Bahrain.

"And the rest of the funds?" the manager said.

The fat man read a new sequence from his notebook. A private bank in the Canary Islands. The manager knew from experience that the half million euros, Baravan Masri's payment for brokering this ransom exchange, would not remain in the Canary account for more than twenty-four hours. It would be dispersed into other secret accounts from one end of the globe to the other.

"*Merci*. And *abientot*," the fat man said. He replaced his notebook in the leather case before buckling it closed. With an effort, he scooted his chair back on the tiles to stand.

The manager did not stand or offer his hand. He watched Baravan waddle to the bank entrance where a uniformed guard held the door open to the furnace heat without.

The young man left his stool in response to the snap of the bank manager's fingers. The manager pointed to the half-full glass resting on his table.

"Shall I take the glass away and wash it, sir?" the boy said.

"No. Throw it away. I never want to see it again," the manager said. He closed his laptop with a snap. He would have his wife draw a bath for him and he would soak for hours. He would try and steam away the filth he imagined now covered him from head to toe.

———

A Red Crescent ambulance screamed west down Highway 2. It weaved around blackened wrecks. Clots of refugees broke up to seek shelter on the verges as it bore down on them. Sniper fire cracked overhead as it closed on the protective berm.

It arrived in the evening at a checkpoint manned by Iranians from the Golden Battalion. After a cursory inspection, the black-clad soldiers waved the Mercedes through and toward the Kurdish safe zone. The ambulance stopped only long enough to allow a woman and two young boys to step out onto the verge of the road. The woman and the boys made their way north along a cracked asphalt road that wound between hills growing purple in the dying light. By full night, they made it to the lights of an aid station at the edge of a refugee processing center.

The aid workers were Danes from an NGO funded through donations gathered from Lutherans all across Europe. They listened to the woman's story. She and her sons were captives of Daesh until that morning. Her husband paid for their release, and they were told to meet him at a Kurdish camp near Ba'ashiqah. A pair of volunteers, a married couple from Esbjerg, offered to drive the woman and her children to her husband the following morning.

The woman slept that night on a cot she shared with her sons. Or, truth be told, she *tried* to sleep. Anxiety over the reunion with her husband kept her awake until the hours just before dawn. For months, she thought of nothing else but seeing Farhad's face again. Now the reality of what that moment might be like troubled her deeply. Every wife likes to believe they know the man they have married. In the isolation of the dark, she questioned her knowledge of the man, allowed doubt to steal away her faith in the man. Her treatment at the hands of Daesh did not break her because she held on to the hope that her life would return one day to what it was. The dismal realization that perhaps nothing could ever be as it seemed created in her heart a loneliness that was almost too painful to bear.

She would bear it for her sons. They slept close by her in the narrow bunk, their breathing easy—the first real sleep they'd had in the weeks since their capture. Her sons were safe now. They had a future once more. If she lost the love of her husband, then she would have to take solace in the salvation of her boys.

And that would be enough for her. She pulled them closer to her, biting back hot tears and stifling sobs.

By the next afternoon, Dersima Aman and her boys were reunited with her husband at Ba'ashiqah. It was as though no moment had passed since the last time they saw one another. Farhad stumbled to his knees to embrace them all, planting kisses on his wife and sons, his eyes streaming with tears. He gathered them to him and whispered a prayer of thanks to God for their return.

Farhad brought Dersima and his sons to meet the man, an American, who made their delivery from bondage. This man paid their ransom somehow. He asked for little in return for his gift.

"What does he want from us?" Dersima said, her eyes

cast down upon meeting the tall, lean man with a fresh scar on his forehead. He looked like a hard man, but with a smile that came easily. His eyes were kind.

"I want nothing but for you to tell me your story. I ask you to be brave and spare no detail in the telling," the American said in halting Kurmanji.

29

"You're weird," Lisa said.

"Why?" Merry looked up from her paperback, the spell of Phillip Marlowe's Los Angeles broken for the moment.

"You run up here after dinner to *read*? Some old *book*?" Lisa crossed their shared room. She shoved the top sash of a window down. She rested a butt cheek on the sill before pulling a fresh pack of cigarettes from a hiding place behind the radiator.

"That's not a good thing to do," Merry said. She squinched her nose.

"You going to tell?" Lisa undid the cellophane and shook the pack to pull a butt free with her lips.

"I'm no tattletale."

"You know how to keep a secret, huh?"

"I keep myself to myself." Merry tried to return to her book. The acrid stink of a struck match was followed by the funk of a tobacco cloud.

"You learn that from your daddy? The outlaw?" Lisa was smiling at Merry. Not in a nice way. She sat balanced on the sill, long skinny legs crossed and the Marlboro between her fingers in imitation of some actress from a movie she'd seen.

"My daddy's not an outlaw. He's a good man."

"Said every criminal's kid ever. I heard Carrie and Greg talking about your 'daddy.'"

"What did they say?"

"They said he's wanted by the police, and nobody can find him. The court turned you over to foster care because once they catch him, he's going to prison forever."

"They don't know anything about my daddy," Merry said. She wanted to say, "They'll never catch him." But that sounded like bragging. And it also sounded like her daddy was never coming back. Only he promised he would, promised he'd always come back. And her daddy never lied to her.

"Well, get used to a shitty life. It only gets worse from here." Lisa blew a stream of smoke through the window screen.

"Why are you so mean?" Merry said.

"Think I'm mean? You don't know shit. You don't know fuck about anything." Lisa's smile quivered at the edges. Her eyes darkened, the sadness in them welling to the surface.

"I was reading," Merry said.

"Fine." Lisa swiped the cigarette across the screen, sending a spray of embers out into the night. She stomped from the room and down the hall. Merry heard the bathroom door squeal shut with a bang.

Merry turned back to the book and the sun-drenched streets of North Hollywood.

———

Merry woke to hushed voices. Someone sat on the edge of her bed, weighing the mattress down. A hand poked her side.

"Hey. Wake up." The voice was a hiss. She opened her eyes. The room was dark.

She sat up suddenly, drawing away from the poking hand.

It was Blaine. The Knox's son. He sat on the edge of her bed. He was shirtless. Across the room Lisa sat up in her bed.

"Leave her alone," Lisa said.

"Shut up," Blaine said, turning to her. He stood and waved Merry from the bed.

"Is something wrong?" Merry looked from Blaine to Lisa. His face was illuminated by the moonlight coming through the window, eyes lifeless as marbles. Lisa's face was hidden in shadow.

"Yeah. We want to be alone and you're here. That's what's wrong. Get out."

"Where do I go?"

"I give a fuck? Go into the bathroom."

Merry looked to Lisa. She saw Lisa's head nod in the dark.

She ran barefoot from the room down the hall to the bathroom and locked herself in. She sat on the edge of the tub in the dark, not sure what to do. Not even sure what to think. Maybe Lisa and Blaine were like girlfriend and boyfriend. Only they didn't act that way. Lisa acted as if she didn't like Blaine. Maybe she was even afraid of him. Now Merry was afraid of him too. A shiver came over her and she

LEVON'S WAR | 135

crossed her arms to hold in her body heat. Only she wasn't cold.

crossed her arms to hold in her body heat. Only she wasn't cold.

Once she asked her father why her mother was gone, why her mother had to die.

"No one can answer that. At least, no one in this world," Levon told her.

"Will we ever know the reason?" she said.

"I like to think that Jesus will explain it all someday. Maybe that's heaven's greatest gift. Knowledge. We'll all know why this or that happened, why it had to happen like it did. Every question we ever had answered."

"How can Jesus answer all those questions?"

"Because he knows all the answers."

"No. No. I mean there's billions of people with jillions of questions. How can he answer them all?"

"Because he has all the time there ever was. And because he loves us."

"What do we do until then?"

"We try and do what's right. The world is filled with trials and God watches how we deal with them."

"Find the answers for ourselves?" Merry said.

"That's right, honey. Best we can," Levon said.

Merry sat on the edge of the tub and prayed. She prayed for the trials to end. She prayed for God to see that she'd had enough of trials and only wanted peace for herself and her father. And Merry prayed for the soul of her mother, Arlene Cade, and hoped that she was with Jesus now. That her mother was through with suffering and had all the knowledge that her father promised was waiting for them all in Heaven. And that the knowledge brought her mother serenity.

A soft rap at the door woke her. She was curled up on the bathmat, though she could not remember lying down there. Merry crept to the door and opened it an inch at a time until she could see the empty hallway. A door closed with a muffled click somewhere down the hall. She padded back to her room. It was fuzzy with gray light coming through the window.

Lisa lay covered up, her face to the wall and back to Merry. A sour smell like old sweat hung in the air. Merry slid into her own bed, the sheets cool. She lay trying to fall back to sleep, listening to the peep and twitter of birds in the trees outside. The gray light turned pink. Shadows stretched across the ceiling.

There was another sound from inside the room.

Lisa was crying, her face crushed into a pillow to hide her sobs. Wet sniffles and a rhythmic mewling in her chest. Merry turned to say something and stopped herself. She recalled their conversation about secrets. Lisa had her own secret to hide, and it was plain that she didn't care to share it.

Merry finally drifted off. She woke up to a clatter of breakfast dishes from downstairs.

Lisa's bed was empty.

30

Dersima Aman's well of tears was dry.

She spoke with mounting anger. Her hands shook. Her husband reached out to hold them still. She pulled her hands from his and pushed at him.

"Please, I will tell this man my story, Farhad. But it is nothing for you to hear. Be with our children."

"I wish to be here with you. To be strong for you," he said. She shook her head, chin high. Her lips were pressed shut. Farhad knew that his wife had said her final word on the subject. He left the medical tent without further protest.

"Thank you for speaking with me," Levon said.

"I only do so because I believe you when you say you are here to rescue someone," she said. Her dark eyes bored into his, searching for the truth there. She saw only immutable resolve and was satisfied. This man was foreign, from a world she would never know. Still, she recognized something in him that was familiar to her. There was a strength there, an honesty.

"You were taken with others from Baiji?" Levon said.

He uncapped a fresh bottle of water and handed it to her. She nodded her thanks, taking the cool bottle, but did not drink.

"Only women and children. And only those who worked for the oil company. And only those who were not Sunni."

"And the Sunnis?"

"They pointed us out. The filthy swine brought them to our door. These men were our neighbors. They worked with my husband. They were to our homes for meals, and we to theirs. But when Daesh came, they betrayed us."

"What happened to the men in Baiji? The ones who weren't Sunni?"

"They shot them. In their kitchens. In their yards. There were dead in the gutters. I saw them. I covered my sons' eyes to protect them, you see? I didn't know they would see much worse very soon. They took us to trucks. They tried to pull my boys from me, but I fought them, cursed them."

"And Pejma Hassan and her daughters?"

"I saw her. She held her girls to her as I held my boys. They pulled her girls away. She fought as well. One of the Daesh struck her over the head with his rifle. She fell. He kept hitting her again and again until her head was crushed. They put the girls in another truck."

"Did you see the girls again?"

"Many times. We were all taken to Mosul. To a stadium there. There were other women with their children. Hundreds. Maybe a thousand. They took pictures of us all. I saw Rona and Kani there until I was taken away by some of the men."

"You don't need to tell me anything about that."

"You are a kind man." Her eyes remained fixed on his face.

"When is the next time you saw the Hassan girls?"

"A few days later. I cannot be sure how long. They brought me to a hotel. I remember staying there once when my husband had business in Mosul. I was together with my boys again. That kept me alive. My boys are everything to me. I would endure Hell for them. Do you understand me? Are you a father?"

"I am. Yes."

"Then you know you would do anything to make your children safe."

"I do, and I have. What about the girls?"

"They shared a room with three men. Arab trash. I would see them often, the girls. I was made to clean rooms, to collect their trash, wash their clothing. They did not trust us to make their food, or I would have poisoned every one of them. I know how."

"And the girls are still there as far as you know?"

"I believe they were there when I was taken to be returned to my husband. I saw them only four days ago."

Levon asked specific questions about the hotel, its location, layout, and every detail about the room the girls were being held in. Dersima Aman shared every detail she could recall about the number of men living in the hotel, the number of captives, entrances, exits, stairwells, and elevators. In her role as a housekeeping slave to an ISIS unit, she was allowed a degree of freedom within the hotel. The emir of the Daesh gang she was held by understood that she would never try to escape as long as her boys were prisoners. More comprehensive layouts and schematics for the Plaza Azur would be available online. But Dersima's account provided vital details that only an eyewitness could provide as to the current conditions on the ground.

"Worse than what they did to me is what they did to my boys," she said, at the conclusion of Levon's questions.

Levon only nodded.

"There was a pool, a swimming pool, at the back of the hotel. It was only half-filled with water. Bad water, brown like shit. Their emir, this animal named Abd al Bari Sarraf, he would kill prisoners by the pool and push them in. Iraqi soldiers. Students. Storekeepers. They would kneel in a line while others pointed cameras at them. He would slit their throats and kick their bodies into that sewer."

Her hands squeezed the water bottle; the plastic crackled in her grip. She lowered her eyes to the floor.

"That animal, that pig, would make my sons wash the blood from his blade. And he would reward them with candy and speak to them of God's will and God's justice. That is the worst. That he made them a part of his corruption, that he tried to take my husband's sons and make them his own."

She brought her eyes back up to Levon's. She was looking past Levon, through him, seeing an image in her mind that was far from where they sat together.

"Will you promise me something?" she said.

"If it's my power," Levon said.

"You are going to bring back the Hassan girls. If you see this Abd al Bari Sarraf, will you kill him for me?"

Levon asked for a detailed description of the man.

"If it's God's will, I will bring him God's justice."

"You are a kind man. But maybe not a good man. Do you understand me? I mean no offense," she said.

"None taken," Levon said.

She handed him back the water bottle, crushed out of shape and warm from her hands.

"I will be with my boys now." She stood and gave him a final nod.

And Levon was alone.

———

Hector sat with Bazît Hassan at a table where the Yazidi and some men from his unit were stripping and cleaning weapons. Russian- and Czech-made AKs. American-made M4s and a SAW.

"Hell of a world," Hector said. He nodded at a girl no older than ten seated with the men. She was loading rounds into magazines.

"It is worse for children. I am afraid they will grow up hard, unforgiving," Bazît said. He slid a long spring into the oiled action of an AK.

"Kids are tough."

"Excuse me, but this is bullshit. You do not know children until you have had your own. The soul of a child is fragile. Americans always look for easy answers."

"What about Arabs?"

"That depends on the Arab." Bazît snapped the action of the rifle back into place with a metallic snap.

"Yeah?"

"There is the Arab who only wants to do business. He works hard and honors his god with his labor. Then there is the lazy Arab, who does little to better his life and blames the world for his troubles. To the first Arab, the Koran is a guide to a better life. To the second, it is a haven for his failures, that excuses his every fault and provides comfort for his hatred. And believe me, there are many more of the latter than the former."

"And what kind are you?"

"I am neither. I am a Yazidi. Kind to my fellow man, attractive to women, and rich in all things. That is why we are hated. Because we are happy. Even in battle." Bazît translated for the others who smiled and nodded.

"Even though you've been denied your homeland?" Hector said.

"We will have it one day. In our hearts, Kurdistan is already real. And the Kurds have always tolerated us. We have lived at peace with them for a thousand years."

"But not the Arabs."

"They call us *Ibadat al-Shayton*. They say we worship the Lord of Hell."

"The peacock angel."

"Yes. Melek Taus." The men around the table bowed their heads at the name.

"The Iraqis will never let you have your own land," Hector said. "Or the Turks or the Persians or the Syrians."

"Iraq," Bazît said and spat. "What is it but the land between Persia and the western sea? It has been a place of violence since the chariot was invented, always ruled by others. The Persian, the Hashemite, the English. Then the Americans. It is a place that only recognizes strength. The leaders in Baghdad are weak fools without respect."

"What about Saddam?"

"He left us alone."

"But he was cruel."

"He was Arab." Bazît shrugged.

"So what will become of Iraq after you have chased ISIS out?" Hector said.

"I do not know. No Yazidi knows. No Kurd knows. We can hope for change, perhaps. Never gratitude but change. Like the Arab is two peoples, Iraq is a place with two sides. It is blessed by empty land and cursed by oil. And oil brings new invaders, and they bring money; the deadliest weapon of all."

"What about the United States?"

"I do not trust the United States. Your George Bush and his son lied to us. Obama ignored us."

"And Levon?" Hector said.

"Levon is a man of his word," Bazît said. He drew back the bolt of the Kalashnikov and released it to slide home with a sharp report.

31

The rain turned the sunny afternoon into early dusk. Merry ran to the Circle K, her book bag held over her head. She was soaked by the time she joined Lisa under the store's awning. The older girl was alone.

"Where are your friends?" Merry said.

"They're not really friends. Just girls I know," Lisa said.

"You're not smoking."

"Like I ever have any money. I bum from them. But they all went straight home from school."

They stood together, three years and a million miles apart, watching the traffic for Carrie Knox. Tires hissed along the wet street. Two men stood talking under the shelter of the steel roof over the gas pumps.

"Are you going to get married?" Merry said.

"What?" Lisa turned to her, eyes slits.

"You and Blaine. You're in love, right?"

"Are you fucking with me?"

Merry recoiled at the bitterness in Lisa's voice as much as the words.

"I hate that piece of shit," Lisa said.

Before Merry could think of a reply, Lisa was off the concrete apron in the front of the store and across the lot. She vanished in the downpour, shoulders hunched. Carrie pulled up soon after. She was irritated that Lisa wasn't there and angrier when Merry told her that Lisa had walked home.

"I'm not drying her clothes if that's what she thinks," Carrie said. She whipped them off the Circle K lot with a blast from her horn.

———

"My mother died of cancer."

Merry was fluttering at the edge of sleep when Lisa's voice woke her.

"What?" she said. She swam back up to consciousness.

"It was two years ago." Their room was dark. The words were disembodied, rising from where Lisa lay on her bed on the other side of the room they shared.

"Mine too," Merry said.

"Yours too, what?"

"My mother died of cancer too. I was little," Merry said.

She heard Lisa swallow. The older girl had been crying, her voice thick.

"It was lymphoma. God, she was so thin. Her skin was like paper the last time I saw her. So white, I could see her veins through it. I didn't recognize her when I saw her. It was like the only part left of her I knew was her eyes."

"What about your daddy?" Merry said.

"Never knew him. It was always just Mama and me. No family. At least no one who cared about us."

"I still have my daddy."

"Yeah? Where is he?"

"He had to go away. But he'll be back. We'll be together again."

"I used to think that. Or I wanted to believe it. I made up stories for myself about how he was rich and famous. Like Johnny Depp or something. And he'd come home someday, and me and him and Mama would all be together, and everything would be so cool."

"My daddy is coming back. He promised."

"People promise all kinds of shit. They don't mean it. If your daddy was really coming back, you wouldn't be here."

Merry wanted to say that her father's promises meant something. That he would be back to get her. That nothing on earth, distance, time, or any living thing could stop her daddy from coming back. She kept the words to herself—no reason to make Lisa feel bad. The older girl was sad enough already.

The dappled light and shadows cast on the ceiling made Merry imagine they were aboard a ship at sea. The creak of tree branches bending to gusts added to the illusion. Rain pelted the window as the wind swept it along in bands of spray that sounded like waves against a hull. Or as she thought they might sound. Her eyelids were getting heavy when Lisa spoke again.

"You must think I'm some kinda whore," she said.

"I don't," Merry said. Though she had only the vaguest notion of what a whore was.

"I don't love him. I don't even like him."

Merry pictured them alone, safe in the hull of a ship on a storm-ravaged sea.

"I never wanted to be with him like that." Lisa spoke through clenched teeth. "I was never like that. Never a bad girl."

"Why do you let him?" Merry said.

"Like I have a choice."

"You could tell Mrs. Knox."

"That her son is fucking me?"

The word scared Merry.

"You don't know what it's like in care," Lisa said. "I've been in four homes in two years. It can be worse than this. A lot worse. And no one gives a shit. Do you know who'd be in trouble if I told someone? Me. That's who."

"There has to be something you can do."

"There's nothing. It's less than a year until I'm eighteen and I'll be out on my own."

"What will you do then?"

"The guidance counselor says I can apply to go to beauty school. You know, cutting hair and doing nails and stuff."

Merry heard the bedposts creak across the room from her. A shadow blocked the watery reflection on the ceiling. Then Lisa was sitting on the edge of Merry's bed, and she touched a hand to her arm.

"I'm sorry I've been mean to you," Lisa said.

"It's okay."

"No. It's a shitty thing to be. You're alone. I'm alone. And you're still just a kid."

"I'll be all right."

"Not if you stay here in this house. Not if you're still here when I'm gone. You have to do whatever you can to make sure you're gone by then."

Lisa's hand tightened on her arm for a second. Then the older girl was gone, back to her bed.

Merry lay for a long while in the quiet and the dark, watching the puddled shadows play above her. Her waking fantasy melded into a dream in which she was swinging in a hammock below the deck of a ship that rocked back and forth. She climbed down from the swinging bunk to find she was alone. On bare feet she found her way up a set of steps to the open deck above. There was a wheel spinning there with no one's hands on the spokes as the ship sailed on toward skies black with angry clouds.

32

Gunny Leffertz said:

"Not every man fits every mission."

"Damn straight I'm coming with you," Hector said.

"You've done your job," Levon said.

Bazît Hassan stood in the sun outside the tent waiting for Levon. A young man with a shaved head, stringy beard, and a face like a clenched fist stood by him. He was Bazît's nephew, his sister's youngest son, and the last of the family to join the Peshmerga. Both Yazidis wore a mix of civilian clothing and military finds. Bazît in a dishdashi robe with an ammo vest belted over it. Hejar, the young man, wore loose trousers and shirt under a patched desert camo tunic. Both men had backpacks and water bottles. They carried Kalashnikov rifles as well, the stocks and metal worn, but shiny with fresh oil.

"I told the boss I'd stick with you, and I'm sticking with you," Hector said.

"Duck's not paying you to get your ass shot off."

"That's my call."

"You got me this far. You don't need to prove anything to me, Hector." Levon rucked up. He slid the canvas sling of his own AK over his shoulder.

"You could use me out there." Hector stepped in front of the open tent flap to block Levon's way.

"You're a liability. You look, walk, and talk like an American. You don't blend. I'd be looking out for you the whole time."

"I don't deserve that. I got you this far, like you said." Hector's eyes turned hard.

"You're a good soldier. Damn good. But you're infantry. You'll always be infantry. And the shit I'm about to get into is outside your experience. The bad guys are going to look you in the eye. And they have to see themselves there. You'll never pull that off."

"Okay. You're right, I guess." Hector dropped his eyes. He began to step aside.

Levon closed with him and grabbed a fistful of Hector's shirt, drawing him closer.

"Bullshit," Levon said, his face inches from Hector's. "You're gonna try to follow me. Don't. I see you on my six I will shoot you."

"Jesus," Hector said.

"Swear to me. Give me your word."

"All right. Christ. You're on your own."

Levon studied Hector's face before releasing him. Hector stepped away, hands up and splayed.

"Has to be that way. I'm not going to say I'm sorry, either."

Levon joined Bazît and the boy. They climbed into the bed of a truck driven by one of the Yazidi women Hector had watched dancing the night before. They drove away south on an angle toward the berm.

Hector watched until they were out of sight behind a rising yellow cloud of dust. He stood in the sun considering for a moment the option of following them. Then Hector recalled the look in Levon Cade's eyes when he promised to shoot Hector. Instead, he went back into the tent and called Duck Withers on his SAT phone to give him the sit-rep. The boss asked when Hector was heading back to SinoChem. Hector asked for a few days more in place. Then he lay back in his cot, wishing he could get drunk.

33

"You need to use the phone? Is something wrong?" Coco said.

"I promised to call my social worker and I keep forgetting," Merry said.

She didn't like lying. Especially to Ms. Booth. Merry didn't want to say that Carrie Knox had strict rules about using the phone. One rule really. No one who didn't have the last name Knox was allowed to use the house phone. Merry wouldn't want her listening in on this call anyway.

"Use the phone in the office. Just hit nine first," Coco said.

Merry took a seat behind the desk and found the telephone among stacks of books. She took Miss Nussbaum's business card out of her bookbag and keyed in the number at the top.

"Domestic relations. Can you hold?"

Before Merry could answer there was a click followed by solemn piano music. She wondered what happened when someone couldn't hold. A recording of a man with a tired voice broke in now and then to thank her for holding and assuring her that her call was important and would be answered soon. The last was interrupted by a buzzing tone and a voice came on the line.

"Domestic relations. How may I direct your call?"

Merry asked for Miss Nussbaum. The line clicked and the piano music returned to be interrupted by a series of buzzes before Miss Nussbaum picked up.

"Ellen Nussbaum, foster care," she said.

Merry reintroduced herself and reminded Miss Nussbaum of the promise that she could call anytime there was a problem.

"Oh, yes. I have a visit with you on my calendar for next week. Just to see how you're doing." Miss Nussbaum's voice was friendly in a brittle way.

"I think you need to come sooner, ma'am."

"You do." There was a touch of annoyance in Miss Nussbaum's voice. Merry pictured her lemony expression.

Merry told her what happened two nights before. Blaine Knox coming into her and Lisa's room and making her leave. Blaine being alone in the room with Lisa. Merry coming back to the room to find Lisa crying.

"You think something inappropriate happened?" Miss Nussbaum said.

"Lisa was very upset, and she was gone early this morning. She told me stuff last night."

"Are Lisa and the Knox boy maybe boyfriend and girlfriend? Maybe they had a fight."

"She says they're not. Lisa's scared of him."

"But you didn't actually *see* anything happening?" Miss Nussbuam pressed hard on the word 'see.'

"I'm not lying, ma'am."

"No. No. I'm not *saying* you're lying, honey. But maybe you didn't understand what you saw. Lisa *is* a few years older than you."

"Maybe. Only Blaine shouldn't be coming into my room when everybody's asleep."

"Have you told Mrs. Knox?"

"No, ma'am."

"And why not?"

"I don't think she wants to hear about it. I thought maybe she'd think I was lying."

"Why would she think that, honey?"

"'Cause Blaine's her son, I guess. She wouldn't want me saying bad things about him."

"Well, I can talk to her. Is that what you want?"

"Yes, ma'am."

"I'll call her later and set up a time to visit. Is that okay with you?"

"Yes, ma'am."

"Thank you for calling and telling me about this, Merry." Miss Nussbaum hung up.

Merry heard Miss Nussbaum's sigh before the connection was broken. She didn't sound grateful at all. Merry set the phone back in its cradle wondering if she'd done the wrong thing. Or maybe the right thing in the wrong way.

———

Carrie Knox said nothing when she picked up Lisa and Merry at the Circle K that afternoon. She drove away without waiting for Blaine. At the house, Lisa jumped out of the car to run to the house. In the back seat, Merry tried the handle on the bay door. It was locked.

"You called Miss Nussbaum," Carrie said. Merry could see her eyes in the mirror on the windshield. They were hard behind the cat's-eye lenses.

"Yes."

"Are you trying to get us in trouble?" Her voice was as hard as her eyes.

"I don't want to get anyone in trouble."

"Well, you're doing a piss-poor job of that. Greg and I take you girls in, and this is the thanks? You telling lies about my son?"

"I didn't lie, ma'am." Merry felt her eyes well up. There was a lump in her throat, but it was a different kind. It burned.

"Don't you like it here?"

Merry said nothing.

"There are worse homes. Believe me; I've heard stories. You're lucky to have been taken in by us. But you wouldn't know that."

Merry turned from the eyes staring at her from the mirror.

"Go to your room and stay there. I don't want to see you again today."

The door latches clunked. Merry tried the handle and it moved down, the bay door sliding open. She ran to the house and up the stairs to her room. A television was on somewhere. Lisa was locked in the bathroom. Merry lay on her back on her bed and watched the play of shadows across the ceiling cast by the trees outside.

Carrie called her a liar, but didn't ask Merry what she and Miss Nussbaum talked about.

Merry knew that meant something. She had no idea what.

34

Gunny Leffertz said:

"Remember to breathe. And never blink."

The line between the coalition and ISIS-held territory outside of Mosul was fluid and ever-changing. Every night, new attacks from either side pushed the no man's land east or west. Sometimes by kilometers and sometimes by meters. Each new gain by Iraqi government forces was a hollow one. The most fanatic Daesh fighters concealed themselves, allowing each new assault to pass them by. Those pockets of insurgents would then cause all kinds of havoc behind every new line drawn in the sand.

That made crossing the frontier between the two opponents a complicated proposition. A target-rich, free-fire environment. Both sides were trigger-happy and drawn to movement in either direction. There were more bullets than food in the region. Everyone, young and old, had a gun and a grudge. Most of them were militias organized more along the lines of street gangs. Any kind of actual trained military, like the Iraqi army backed by Iranians, was hanging back in the early days of the siege. So, the fighting was mostly hot and furious shooting sprees followed by long periods of silence.

The land between the two sides was tricked out with mines and IEDs. Every square foot was zeroed in for artillery and mortar barrages. Aircraft looking for targets of opportunity were constantly on the prowl in the skies above. A trio of unidentified men on foot near the ISIS lines would be irresistible in this shoot first/pray later land where payback was Job One.

Levon lay in the shelter of an abandoned farmhouse. He leaned right to take a turkey peek through a hole in the masonry, made weeks before by a round fired by a tank. The land to the west was all lines and shadows as the sun dropped behind a rank of heights. A gray haze from diesel fires was beginning to stir in breezes created over the cooling ground. He moved back into the part of the house that was still covered by the collapsed roof. Bazît and Hejar waited in the shadows.

"We move as soon as it gets full dark," Levon said. "What lies ahead from here?"

"Highway 2 is out of sight over those hills." Bazît pointed south. "The Gogjali road is to the north. We stay between them until they join just outside the city at a collection of houses."

"My father brought me here sometimes," Hejar said. "We would stop here when he had business in Mosul.

This was a date farm. They had ponies and sometimes he paid to let me ride one." The young man spoke without regret or nostalgia.

"Where is your father now?" Levon said.

"Dead. Killed by Daesh," the boy said. Something bitter came into his voice.

"I'm going to keep watch until we move. You two do whatever you have to do to get ready," Levon said.

"What story will you tell, Levon? So that we will know if we are asked. What brings a European to fight for the caliph?" Bazît said.

"I'm a Chechen drawn to Daesh to kill Russians."

"Do you speak Chechen?"

"No. My Russian is fluent."

"And if we happen to encounter any Chechens?"

"You always think of the worst."

"That is why I am alive," Bazît said.

"I'll let you know when it's dark enough to move."

———

The night above was streaked now and then by arcs of glowing tracers chasing one another against the stars. The ripping sound of small arms punctuated by the freight train chug of heavier weapons. There were no sustained engagements. The rounds were going off along the sky to the north and south without rhythm or reason. Just random bursts of fire sent out by the anxious or bored.

Hejar knew the country best and moved ahead on point. Levon and Bazît followed at intervals. The boy led them on a path that kept to the lowest parts of the terrain for minimum exposure. Sometimes crouched, sometimes crawling, they passed within yards of fixed positions of gunners dug into improvised bunkers of earth and rubble. Within a few hours they were well behind the fluid eastern border of the caliphate.

There were rooftops visible ahead. Levon let out a low whistle. Hejar turned to see the American pointing to the south toward the highway.

At a casual walk, they approached a place on the highway blocked by an improvised barricade constructed from sheets of corrugated metal and a bullet-scarred bus. The road surface was littered with empty shell casings. Hejar's head was on a swivel, turning left and right. His hands were tight on his rifle. Levon drew alongside him.

"Walk as though we belong here," Levon said. "Act like you would when you came to Mosul with your father."

The boy turned to him, beads of sweat gleaming silver on his brow beneath the keffiyeh that rested on his head.

Levon threw an arm around him and drew him close. He put his mouth close to the boy's ear and spoke low.

"There are eyes on us. Guns too. Do you have balls of steel or balls of cheese?" he said.

"Steel," Hejar said through clenched teeth.

Levon laughed aloud and slapped the boy across the back of the head. Bazît turned at the sudden sound. He barked a laugh at the unusual sight of his friend's open amusement. Even Hajar was smiling as a voice called to them from the barricade.

"What is so funny?" A high-pitched voice from the makeshift barricade. The accent was Egyptian Arabic.

They kept on toward the barricade at an effortless walk. Bazît nodded his head toward Hajar.

"The boy said he is hungry. My friend said he would feed him soon. Then the boy said he was horny as well. My friend said, 'then eat the ass of the goat last.'" Bazît wore a broad grin.

"Why is the boy not laughing?" the voice called.

"I guess he doesn't like goat." Bazît shrugged.

There were chuckles from behind the barricade. A man climbed to the roof of the rusted bus and waved them to the left of the barricade toward a ditch at the side of the roadway.

The way to Mosul was open.

———

The sun was up and baking the concrete surface of the highway from Gogjali. Vultures perched on power lines that paralleled the roadway. The ragged remnants of bodies hung from wire nooses slung over the bars of the towers. They wore signs about their necks proclaiming them to be enemies of the caliphate, heretics, and traitors to the Word of the Prophet.

Levon, Bazît, and the boy walked in a column along the dusty verge. The city lay before them, the buildings shimmering in the growing heat haze. A column of black smoke from a recent air sortie rose into the sky. As they neared the eastern edge of Mosul, they were challenged by men who stepped from behind a pickup truck.

It was Bazît who told the men that they were separated from the rest of their unit during a firefight along the frontier.

"Who are you with?" The man's voice was muffled by

a black mask drawn over his face. The others wore black headscarves covering all but their eyes.

"The Nahawand Brigade. Have you seen any of us who have returned this way?" Bazît said.

"Not this morning," the black mask said.

"Maybe they will come along later."

"Or they are martyrs."

"*Inshallah.*" Bazît bowed his head. "It is God's will."

The masked men offered them a ride into Mosul. Levon and Bazît exchanged a look. Levon nodded.

They rode in the bed of the truck seated upon the uneasy cargo of ammo crates and boxes of RPG projectiles. The truck plowed ahead at top speed, winding a serpentine course around craters in the road surface and scorched piles of wrecked vehicles. To the north were walled and gated compounds of mini mansions with white rooftops set well off the highway. To the south, the close-packed apartment houses stacked cheek by jowl to the edge of the road.

The morning call to prayer could be heard through the cones of loudspeakers slung along the roadway atop utility poles. The rising and falling of the muezzin's voice was punctuated by the honks and squeals of feedback.

Riding with them was a skinny kid with an iPad knockoff held against his knees. Only his eyes were visible through the slit of the headscarf tied about his face. The comic book villain effect of the mask was spoiled by a pair of eyeglasses perched on his nose. An unpopped zit the size of a corn kernel in the fold of his nose. His fingers danced over the screen with a life of their own. He glanced up at Levon.

"You are not Arab," the skinny kid said.

"I am Chechen. Argun Varyev is my name," Levon said.

"You came to fight for the Islamic State?"

"*Alhamdo lillah.* It is the duty of all the faithful."

The kid's eyes dropped to the screen as he stabbed at it with a finger. Levon looked sideways to Bazît riding across from him. The Yazidi's face appeared to be disinterested in the conversation. The grip on his rifle tightened, the skin across his knuckles stretched thin. Hejar looked from the skinny kid to Levon with eyes narrowed to slits.

"What does this fight mean to a Chechen?" the skinny kid said.

"What does it mean to you? To kill infidels. To bring glory to the Lord. To make a land from which the word might spread to all the world."

"You hate infidels?"

"I hate Russians." Levon hawked and sent a gob of spit over the side of the truck.

"There are no Russians in Iraq."

"I hope to go to Raqqa. There are Russians there."

The kid's fingers tapped at the screen on his knee.

"You are with Nahawand?" the skinny kid said.

"We fight for Yarub al Khattoni. We die for him if he so asks."

"Where in the city are you going?"

"The Nineveh Governate. But you do not need to drive us that far, my friend."

The skinny kid tilted his head and shifted the tablet in his hands to draw his finger down the screen. Levon pretended to be interested in a shelled-out apartment block. Children in filthy clothing were sorting through rubble.

"You are lying," the skinny kid said, eyes large behind the thick lenses.

He returned the tablet to an open pouch on his ammo vest. With the flat of his hand, he drummed on the fender and called out to his brothers in the truck cab.

35

Merry got up extra early in the morning to eat breakfast, a bowl of Raisin Bran, and prepare her lunch. A peanut butter and honey sandwich and a banana. The house was quiet. It wouldn't be for long. Merry started up the stairs to take her bath and dress for school. She met Carrie coming down.

"Where are you going?" she said.

"Getting ready for school?" Merry said.

"You won't be going to school today."

"Why not? What happened?"

"Nothing happened. You're sick."

"But I feel fine."

Carrie, face crimson, came down the stairs toward her. Merry stumbled back a step, gripping the banister. Carrie took her by the arm.

"You'll do as you're told. Go to your room." She released Merry's arm, leaving pallid finger marks on the skin. Merry ran past her and up the steps.

Lisa was in the room getting dressed for school. She was picking clothes from an array spread across her bed.

She had on jeans and a bra and was in the process of deciding between a blouse or a T-shirt.

"What did you do? Carrie's mad at me too," Lisa said.

"Are you really not Blaine's girlfriend?" Merry said.

"What?"

"Are you in love with him?" Merry leaned back on her bed and rubbed her arm where Mrs. Knox had gripped her.

"I told you about that. Why are you still asking me?" Lisa flushed red from her neck until her face was scarlet.

"I told the lady at foster care what happened."

"Jesus!" Lisa looked stricken. She turned away.

"But if he's your boyfriend then I'm sorry and—"

"Shut up! Shut your mouth!" Lisa shouted. She scooped up a top and her bookbag and rushed into the hall.

Merry lay back on her bed and tried to read one of the books Ms. Booth loaned to her. She read the same page over and over again, but it made no sense to her. She gave up and set the paperback aside to stare at the ceiling. There was a breeze moving the branches of the tree outside the window. Overlapping shadows in shades of gray played across the plaster. The breezes made a brushing sound against the screen.

A clicking sound made Merry sit up from the bed. She'd dozed off without realizing it. Her stomach growled and she thought of the sandwich and banana she'd left downstairs on the kitchen counter. She was surprised to see the bedroom door was shut now. Even more so to find it locked. She bent to look into the keyhole. No light came through from the hallway. There was a key in the hole. The clicking sound she heard.

Merry lay back on the bed and wondered what Philip

Marlowe would do. Probably, he'd take a drink and ponder his place in the universe. She thought Mike Hammer might be more useful right now. He'd rush the door with his shoulder and smash it open.

Tires crunched to a stop at the curb out in front of the house. Merry went to the window. Miss Nussbaum's car. Merry stepped back from the window to watch Miss Nussbaum step from the car, a leather case under her arm, and walk out of sight to the front door. Merry dropped down to press an ear to the carpet. The bell rang below. Footsteps. The door opened. Muffled voices. Carrie and Miss Nussbaum.

Merry found a copy book on Lisa's nightstand and tore a page from it. There were some hairpins on the vanity they were supposed to share but mostly Lisa used. Merry knelt by the door and pushed the sheet of paper out into the gap under the door until it was beneath the doorknob. She bent the hairpin straight and fished it into the keyhole. If the key was turned in the lock she was stuck. But she felt it begin to give. She poked gently until the key dropped from the hole onto the hall floor outside the door.

With her fingertips flat, she drew the sheet of copy paper back toward her under the door. A copper-colored key was resting on the paper. She took it and unlocked the bedroom door and, slow as she could, pushed the door open to creep into the hall on stocking feet. At the banister at the top of the stairs she stopped. The voices of the two women came up to her from the living room below.

"—there's no foundation for what she told me?" Miss Nussbaum.

"She made something out of nothing. That's all it is." Carrie's voice.

"She *was* light on details."

"Like I told you, Lisa borrowed a CD from Blaine, and he came in the room to ask her to return it. Merry was asleep. She woke up and saw them talking and thought—I don't know what she thought."

"You understand that I need to respond to these calls."

"Absolutely."

"It's a sensitive situation. You have a teenage boy living at home. And a female foster child around the same age."

"I know. Hormones, right? But we keep a strict house here. There's nothing between Blaine and Lisa. I would know."

"And Merry is in school right now?"

"Yes. She is. I'm leaving in a half hour to pick her and Lisa up to bring them home."

Merry's hands tightened on the banister rails.

"Okay. I guess there's no need to talk to her again before my scheduled visit next week."

"I'm sure she's sorry she's caused you so much trouble."

The women were moving now, the words they spoke lost to Merry as they both moved to the front door. Merry was up and running, as fast as she could without making noise, back to the bedroom. She reached the window in her room as the front door shut below her. She watched Miss Nussbaum walk down the pavement to her car. Merry shoved the window open.

"Miss Nussbaum," Merry said through the screen.

There was a hitch in Miss Nussbaum's step. Her shoulders went rigid.

"Miss Nussbaum, please," Merry said again through the window.

Miss Nussbaum kept on to her car.

"Up here," Merry said, louder this time.

Before getting in her car Miss Nussbaum turned for a second, her eyes fell on Merry pressed to the screen above. She turned back and slid behind the wheel and drove away.

"Haven't you made enough trouble?" Carrie Knox was in the doorway, eyes slits and her mouth a cruel, lipless line.

"You lied," Merry said.

"You lied first." Carrie took the key from the inside lock and closed the door. The lock clicked closed and Merry heard the key slide from the cylinder.

36

Gunny Leffertz said:

"You have to know when to throw in a shit hand."

Levon hit the skinny kid with a double tap to the chest. The kid spilled over the side of the truck and tumbled on the concrete, limbs flailing.

Bazît fired his rifle at the same time, sending a long burst into the rear wall of the truck cab. The figures inside jerked forward under the impact. The truck slewed to the left, hopping a sand median, slowing as the driver's lifeless foot slipped from the accelerator. The engine choked and the truck rolled to a full stop with the nose pointing down into a ditch that ran along the foot of a block wall.

Bazît had leaped clear as the truck died, and Hejar just behind him. They dragged gear and packs with them as they spilled to the dust. Levon stayed in the truck until it came to rest. He climbed out, his backpack slung loosely over one shoulder. He waved them away. The Yazidis ran along the wall to a gate and ducked inside. Levon backed away from the truck. He pulled the pin from an HE grenade and tossed it in an underhand loop into the bed of the truck.

He was nearly to the gate in the wall when the grenade went off with a pop followed by the deeper boom of an RPG exploding. More rounds went off in near-simultaneous succession creating a concussive ring of force that knocked Levon to his knees. His backpack swung to slap him across the side of the head. Spinning bits of molten metal made whistling sounds over him. He continued at a crawl and was helped through the open gateway by Bazît and Hejar's hands pulling at his clothing. A new detonation sent the stalled truck skyward in two pieces. This blast raised dust off the rooftops of the homes behind the wall. The men were up and running by then, vanishing into the warren of closely packed apartment buildings.

Automatic fire erupted immediately from all around them. Tracers arced through the morning sky. The blast started a blocks-wide fusillade of return fire at an imagined enemy. The jihadis' buck fever was in full effect and every finger found a trigger, firing without question or reason in any and all directions. Tracers soared into the morning sky in search of imagined infidel aircraft.

Taking full advantage of the noisy chaos, Levon led his friends in a charge down alleys and across courtyards and gardens. When faces appeared at windows and doorways, he shouted warnings in Arabic that the infidels were here. The final fight was upon them, and Allah be praised.

The noise of one-sided combat died away behind them as they emerged from the maze of backstreets into an open area that might have been a pocket park at one time. Now it was just dust with patches of grass scorched brown by the sun. Stumps dotted the ground; all that remained of trees cut down for firewood. Some kids were kicking a partly deflated soccer ball across the trash-strewn lot. Pedestrians moved along the walks, deaf to the sounds of war only a few blocks north. The foot traffic was all one-way. It was also populated by men only. Many of them were armed. Levon and his comrades fell in with the flow. The human tide would take them to a marketplace or mosque where they could more easily blend in.

The walk to the market took a winding path around streets choked with the rubble of buildings collapsed by months of pinprick air strikes by the coalition. The wet ash smell of smoldering fires was everywhere. And under it, the corrupted stench of rotting flesh. No one was working to find the dead under the ruins of apartment blocks and storefronts. Some of the homes they passed were marked in spray paint with a symbol that looked like a one-eyed smiley face.

"What does that mean?" Levon said.

"It is how Daesh marks the homes of infidels or undesirables," Bazît said.

"What happened to them?"

"They convert to Islam, to Sunni. Or they pay the *jizya*, the tax paid by unbelievers."

"What happens if they can't pay it? Or run out of money?"

"They die. Their women are taken away to be brides of the faithful. Their children are slaves," Bazît said.

There were posters and paintings, some comically crude, of the new caliph on the walls of buildings. Abu Bakr al Baghdadi's face was everywhere, scowling down from under his ever-present black cap. His was the face of power and oppression. He was the *mahdi* of this new malignant movement. Not for a moment was the population of the city allowed to forget this. In addition to his constant image was his voice echoing from speakers and radios everywhere, a reminder that the people of Mosul were prisoners in their own homes. These were taped harangues that ran on loops day and night. They offered the faithful the pleasures of paradise in Heaven and the satisfaction of justice on Earth. They promised apostates a dishonorable death followed by an eternity in hell.

Further evidence of the hold ISIS had over the city was the increased presence of jihadis in uniforms of black and desert camo. They loitered everywhere, seated in the shade of doorways, smoking in groups all around the souk.

The market itself was a sad affair. Every stall that offered food was crowded ten deep with men waving fistfuls of near-worthless cash. The tables had little to offer in the way of fresh food. Merchants had battered case lots of canned goods and surplus American MREs. Small shrunken carcasses hung in rows from lines. Deep-fried rats and pigeons. There were plastic jugs of cloudy drinking water and baskets of pistachios with rust-colored hulls.

More plentiful than edibles were weapons. Every description of firearm was on display, along with pallet loads of ammunition, all marked with stamps of the United States Army or stencils in Cyrillic lettering. Also body armor, webbing, boots, and all manner of ordnance. All taken from the stores of the Iraqi army when they fled the city under threat of the less than a thousand ISIS fighters who took Mosul for the Islamic State.

Also in abundance were books. These stalls saw the least business. Only a few white-whiskered browsers sorted through the stacks.

The mood of the souk was subdued. The usual cacophony of overlapping conversation was gone. The sound of discourse, laughter, haggling, and conversation was muted, constrained.

Levon and Bazît found a place to sit in the shade of a tattered awning before a shuttered restaurant. They sent Hejar into the throng of hagglers at the food stalls. He returned with a gallon plastic bag of watered-down apricot juice and a greasy bag of rat kebobs.

"Rat is disgusting," Bazît said. He peeled a strip of crackled flesh and inspected it.

"Rat, rabbit, or Kobe beef. It all tastes good if you're hungry enough. But some habanero helps," Levon said. He dug into a pocket and came up with a tiny dark glass bottle. He sprinkled a dot or two on his rat and handed it off to the others.

Hejar made approving noises as he munched the flavored meat. They ate the kebobs and shared the bag of juice until it was dry. They sat a while and talked, their conversation hidden under the ambiance of voices in the market.

"The Plaza Azur is on the other side of the river. We need to cross before dark," Levon said.

"Before we do that, you need to come up with new lies, friend," Bazît said.

"My Chechen cover has some holes," Levon said.

"How did that bastard know you were lying?" Bazît said.

"Google," Hejar said around a mouthful of rat.

37

The door to the room was unlocked when Lisa got home from school. Merry brushed past her to run to the bathroom. She thought her bladder would burst after spending all day shut in the room.

Carrie Knox was there when she came out of the bathroom.

"Can I trust you to stay in your room?" Carrie said.

"Yes," Merry said.

"Without locking you in?"

"Yes. Can I have something to eat?"

"I'll bring something up when I get a chance." Carrie walked her back to the room.

Lisa had already changed clothes. She didn't look at Merry.

"Going out," she said and tromped away down the stairs.

"Have you thought about trying to get along here?" Carrie said from the doorway.

"Yes," Merry said.

"No more phone calls? No more troublemaking?"

"Yes."

"I'll be back with a sandwich for you."

"Thank you."

Carrie pulled the door shut behind her. The lock did not slide into place. She returned within an hour with a PB&J, an apple, and a glass of milk.

"Will I be able to come down for dinner?" Merry said, taking the plate and glass and setting them on the vanity.

"I don't think that's such a great idea," Carrie said.

"Can I take a shower later?"

"Yes. Before bedtime."

"Okay."

The door closed and Merry was alone again. She ate by the window, watching some kids riding bikes up and down the sidewalk.

———

Lisa was the next one to come to the door. It was night outside.

"Carrie said you could take a shower, but then you have to go right to bed."

"I'm sorry," Merry said.

"Just stop talking to me. Stop talking to anyone."

Lisa went down the stairs.

Merry gathered her pajamas and left the room. The hall was quiet except for the sound of the TV from the living room below: muffled voices and the laughter of an audience. The doors along the hall stood open, the rooms dark.

She locked the bathroom door and turned the shower on. While the water warmed, she brushed her teeth, rinsing out the toothbrush and setting it aside.

The hot spray felt good on her face. She felt itchy after a night and a day spent cooped up in the room with only her borrowed paperbacks and the view from the window for distractions. She washed her hair and scrubbed her body and then spent a long while just letting the water fall across her shoulders. Carrie would probably complain about all the hot water she was using up. Merry didn't care. Cocooned here in the steamy air, scented with the astringent smell of shampoo, she felt alone in the world. The shower curtain formed a barrier to the world outside. She even hummed part of a song she'd heard on Carrie's car radio the day before.

The water was beginning to cool and she turned the tap off. She reached a hand through the curtain for a towel she'd left draped on the rack. It wasn't there. She ran fingers up and down the bar, but the towel was gone, probably slipped to the floor. Merry parted the curtain to step onto the bathmat and froze, one foot in and one foot out of the tub.

Blaine was leaning against the sink counter, her towel in one hand.

"You looking for this?" he said. He held the towel out to her.

She reached for it, and he pulled it back.

"You been talking about me."

Merry said nothing. She drew the shower curtain about her.

"It's none of your fucking business what Lisa and I do," he said. His mouth was twisted in an ugly scowl.

"She doesn't love you," Merry said. Her voice sounded small to her.

Blaine laughed at that. It was a hawking sound and he stifled it with the back of his hand, his eyes still on her.

"You're a skinny little bitch, aren't you? No titties at all." He tossed the towel to her. She let it fall to the floor, staying to the scant cover of the sheer shower curtain.

"Just shut up about me. You don't want my kind of trouble." He turned to go, his back to her. She hurried to bend and scoop up the towel.

He turned back. She retreated into the tub, the towel clutched to her neck.

"Or maybe you do want some of my kind of trouble." His lips formed a crooked smile. He reached a hand for her and laughed again when she stepped away to place her back to the tiled wall. Blaine flicked his fingers at her and turned to leave the room. The door snicked shut behind him.

Merry sank to her knees in the tub, hugging the towel to her.

She wished her daddy was here. She prayed hard for his return, right now, tonight. She made a whispered plea for her father to come through the bathroom door, gather her up in his arms, and take her away from this place.

Only her daddy was far away, and no one was coming to take her from this house.

She was all alone in the world.

No one was going to save her but herself.

38

Gunny Leffertz said:

"The shit you'll see."

They reached the east bank of the Tigris by late morning. They followed a river road south toward the closest bridge, the first of five that crossed the river to the main part of the city. The Al Shohada Bridge was a functionally ugly concrete structure. Four lanes across. A crowd was formed at the center of the span. A periodic roar rose from them and echoed over the slow-moving current of the muddy river. Like a tide, it went up and down in volume as voices joined in response to an electronic hail.

Hejar walked to the edge of the bank. He pointed to a barge anchored in the shadow of the bridge. A lift crane was moving on the deck of the barge. The roar of the mob on the bridge grew in volume each time it swung out to lower its load into the river.

They made their way up onto the bridge span and to the edge of the crowd where they could look down on the barge bobbing in the slow current. The gathering was all male. Men old and young. There were children as well. They lined the edge of the bridge, kneeling at the feet of the adults, leaning out for a better view. Two little boys squatted close to Levon's leg. They nudged each other and pointed, making remarks to one another as though watching a circus parade.

Down on the deck of the barge, a row of men in orange jumpsuits knelt in a row. Their hands bound behind them. Heads lowered. Other men, clad all in black and masked, moved free on the deck. One of them spoke into a hand mike wired to a radio transmitter slung about his shoulder. His voice squawked from speakers mounted atop the barge's wheelhouse. He strode back and forth making grand gestures with his free hand. He harangued the watching faces above with quotes from the prophet. Dire warnings to any who denied the will of God. They would share the fate of heretics and infidels. They would pay the price on Earth and in Paradise. They would be scourged from the caliphate. Their blood would wash the Islamic State clean.

The crane engine rumbled and popped. The chain went taut and was drawn up into the drum. A steel cage rose from the tawny water to swing dripping over the river. On the floor of the cage was a sodden crimson lump. With a squeak the cage was swung inboard and caught by some of the jihadists. It was drawn over the gate and a lever pulled, opening the bottom of the cage like a trap. The cargo dropped to the boards. They used steel hooks to tug the pile apart. It was three men clad in orange jumpsuits like the kneeling men. Their faces were forever locked in open-mouthed masks, eyes bulging, as they'd drowned in the cage. The corpses were dragged to the end of the barge and dropped into the water. Levon watched as they floated, turning in the current, to bump along the hull of the barge before disappearing into the shadows beneath the bridge.

The crowd on the bridge moved in nervous anticipation as three more men in orange were yanked to their feet and walked to the open cage now resting on the deck. The jihadi on the mike recounted the crimes the men were accused of.

"This man, this man worships the false prophet called the Christ! Maybe his God will help him walk on water this day!"

The men along the bridge responded with catcalls and laughter.

The jihadi with the mike held another man's head back by the hair and turned him to face up at the audience above. The man's face was white with terror.

"And this creature lays with other men! He has already watched his lover go into the cage! Should he be shown God's mercy?"

The crowd roared its answer.

The third captive was dragged to the cage. His bare soles slid on the greasy deck as he tried to plant his feet in place. A fist plowed into his back above the hip. He stumbled forward. The jihadi on the mike pointed a damning finger.

"Here we have a usurer! He pretends to be loyal to

Islam, but treats his brothers as a Jew would! Will his money save him from Allah's wrath?"

This drew the loudest response from the men lining the bridge. They shrieked and spat. They shook fists and voiced their fury. Levon saw faces turn red with rage, eyes rolling wild as animals in the throes of a killing frenzy.

The cage was loaded with the three condemned men and the lock put in place. With a bark of exhaust, the crane motor revved up to lift the cage from the deck and spin it out over the water. The operator worked the levers to drop the cage toward the water a foot at a time. As the cage sank into the swirling flow the men climbed the mesh of the cage to stay above the water. The chain was jerked by the current and the cage descended at a canted angle. The men inside began to claw and climb over one another for remaining space within the cage that was still above the water. This only made the angle of the cage more acute. The faces of the condemned were those of feral beasts as they fought for the final breaths they would take in this life.

The crowd reacted like fans at a sporting event. They shouted mock encouragement to the struggling men. Vile insults rained down on them until the cage finally disappeared under the murky stream. There was a hush as the men watched the flurry of air bubbles turn to a feeble spray and then die away to nothing.

Cheers erupted as the cage was hauled up once again to reveal its dripping cargo.

Levon turned away then to walk westward along the bridge. Bazît and Hejar silently followed. The rise and fall of human voices in unison still reached them even when the bridge was out of sight. A shared moan told them that the last of the captives had been fed into the Tigris. The audible sigh of disappointment was followed by a series of celebratory streams of gunfire sent into the afternoon sky.

They picked their way along a lane partly blocked by the rubble of a building collapsed by a coalition JDAM. They passed beneath an enormous black flag hanging over a street on steel cables. Looted homes and ransacked stores lined the streets. The cyclops smiley face symbol was everywhere in this part of the city.

"Kurds lived here once," Bazît said, breaking the quiet shared by the three men.

"What brings men to do such things?" Hejar said.

"This is when men settle scores. When there is no law. This is when they show their true faces," Bazît said.

"Mosul was not always like this, was it? These men were neighbors. They must have lived at peace."

"Without law, there is no peace."

"They have law. They call their law Sharia," Hejar said.

Bazît hawked and spat.

"Sharia is law without order," Bazît said. "Did you see a judge at the bridge? Even an imam? That is not law. It is men justifying their basest desires within a mockery of law. They torture. They kill. They rape. And it is all validated by something they call law when it is only their own desires bared naked."

"They should all die," the boy said. His face grew tighter with his conviction.

"And how should they die? At the end of a rope? A blade across their throats like sheep? Or maybe drowned in a cage in a shitty river?" Bazît said.

The boy lowered his head. His mouth was a tight line,

lips pressed together. His pace slowed and he fell behind the other two men. They made their way along the growing shadows cast by the walls of the urban canyons that grew deeper the closer to the center of Mosul they came.

Levon kept his thoughts to himself. In his mind's eye he could see the faces of those boys, younger than Merry, their eyes eager with bloodlust.

39

It was late in the night. The TV downstairs was quiet. The house was dark.

Lisa was asleep. Her regular breathing interrupted now and then by a mewling deep in her throat. She was dreaming. In her dream she was speaking to someone in a conversation held somewhere beyond the wall of sleep.

Merry could not sleep, and was afraid to dream.

She'd been afraid before. She'd been in trouble before. This time was different. No one was there to help her. No one to listen. No one to care. She was abandoned.

This fear was worse because she didn't know what was to come next. The fear all the more gripping because the days ahead were unknown. All of her life had been spent around adults who she believed were there to protect and guide and love her. Now she was in a world where the adults were only concerned with their own desires. Mrs. Knox and Miss Nussbaum were supposed to be her guardians, and they only wished that she would be silent about what went on in this house. Neither of them protected Lisa from Blaine. And, if it came to that, they would not protect Merry.

Each time she closed her eyes she could see Blaine. His mocking gaze. His wicked smile. She stared at the ceiling and forced her thoughts elsewhere. Her mind fled to better times, happier days.

It had been a cold day in the woods. Not a bitter cold. The sun cut the chill where it came down through gaps in the trees that lined the long gravel drive down from Gunny Leffertz's cabin, deep in the Mississippi pines. She joined him on his daily walk down to the battered mailbox that sat where the drive met the roadway. Merry never missed these walks. She was fascinated at how Gunny could manage the path with such assurance. No one who did not already know would ever have suspected that he was totally blind. She never took his hand. Never felt she should offer him help. He didn't need it.

Most days they walked in silence, listening to the sounds of the woods. Gunny would break the quiet only to identify noises he heard in the trees; noises Merry would never have paid attention to, never noticed, without his help. Gunny would stop and tilt his head toward the source, holding a hand up for her to stop. Together they would stand, ears reaching out into the shadows under the pine boughs. And Gunny would whisper to her the identity of the animal they heard. The chirrup of a red squirrel. The stamp of a deer's hoof. The curious yipping bark of a raccoon.

And some days they would talk. Conversations prompted by questions from Merry.

"Have you ever been afraid, Gunny?"

"Afraid of what, honey?"

"Anything."

"Oh, sure. Lots of times."

"I thought you'd never be afraid of anything."

"Well, there's all kinds of fear."

She walked at his side as he considered his next words.

"There's fear of things you can't change and a fear of things you can change. The first one you can't do anything about. Getting sick. Losing a loved one. God's wrath. We all live with being scared like that. Everyday worries. It's the unknown, stuff bigger than us. No shame in healthy respect for that kind of fear."

"What about the other fear?" Merry said.

"Being afraid of what you *can* change. Letting someone or something scare you. Letting them get the better of you or someone you care about and being so scared you think you can't do anything about it."

"I don't understand."

"Well, some folks don't like the dark. They could light a light and chase the dark away. Then their fear is gone. The real trick is shaking off that fear *without* lighting that light. Only, so many people let that fear inside and can't see a time when that fear is gone. It takes root 'cause they let it. They don't do anything to make themselves strong against it. They let it own them."

"Was my daddy ever scared of anything?"

"Your daddy jumped out of airplanes without hesitation. Live fire exercises, rock climbing, escape training, jungle, desert, arctic maneuvers. I was with him through all of them, ragging on his ass the whole way to do better, move faster, and fight harder. And Levon took it all like a weekend on a Florida beach."

"He was never afraid of any of that?"

"Water. Your daddy did not like the water. Wasn't used to it. A hillbilly who'd never seen the ocean. It was the Big Unknown to him. That was him being afraid of the dark."

"What did he do?"

"Went through BUDs training with the SEALs. That's the toughest you can get. He had to face it then, look straight into that fear and do what he had to do. Those sailors don't play, honey. They threw him in the deep end of the ocean, and he *lived* there until all that fear was gone. Dunked him down deep with his wrists and ankles tied. Sank him down where the only line between living and dying was the air in his lungs. Ever see your daddy go swimming?"

"He's like a fish."

"See what I mean? His fear of drowning was something he could change, and he changed it."

"Is he afraid of anything else?"

"Honey, I think your daddy's greatest fear is if something were to ever happen to you."

They had come to the mailbox and Merry retrieved the letters, a catalog, and a magazine that were tucked inside. They began the walk back up to the cabin, invisible in the trees around a curve in the drive.

"Is there anything that you're afraid of, Gunny?"

"Broccoli."

Merry giggled.

"Yeah. Joyce took some flounder out of the freezer for tonight and she always serves it with damn broccoli. I can smell it from here."

Joyce was Gunny's wife of many years and a retired Marine herself.

"It makes your pee smell funny too," Merry said.

"There's that, too. Awful stuff."

Gunny took her hand then, something he'd never done before on one of their walks. They walked awhile like that, neither saying a word.

"Sometimes all it takes to change your world is courage. And I'm an expert on courage. It's my religion. I preach it from my pulpit. I think you get a whole lot of courage from your daddy." He gave Merry's hand a squeeze that she returned.

The memory faded there, leaving only the warmth of Gunny's hand on hers. She was out of the sunlit woods now and back in the dark of her borrowed room.

Merry lay listening to the regular sound of Lisa's breathing. She released her grip on the sheets. She made fists of her hands. She thought about what she could change.

40

Gunny Leffertz said:

"You have to believe your own bullshit. That's the only way bullshit works."

The Plaza Azur maintained some of its former staid elegance. But only at a distance. The signs of the recent occupation were more apparent as Levon and the two other men got closer.

Once the jewel of the high-end foreign hotels that lined Nineveh Street in the Abu Tamamam sector, the Azur was now a fortress. Barriers of sandbags and rubble were heaped before the entrances in untidy piles. The grand wall of windows that once lined the ground floor had been filled in with crudely laid blocks and mortar. All of the walls on street level were covered in graffiti quoting either the Koran or the new caliph. Most of the upper-level glass was either fractured or entirely blown out—the result of air strikes on nearby targets. A banner, four stories in length, was draped down one face of the building. Already faded, it featured a painting of Abu Bakr al Baghdadi scowling, his eyes looking down at the street below as if in dark judgment of all who passed beneath. The execution was earnest but amateurish. The caliph's image looked slightly cartoonish, the overall effect that of a velvet painting sold at a gas station. Another face of the building featured an enormous ISIS flag that rippled in the wind from the river.

The French staff and management were long gone. They were replaced by sullen young men lounging against vehicles and seated under the tattered awnings where tourists once enjoyed alfresco dining. They smoked and talked and listened to Sufi pop from a radio wired to a car battery.

The day was dying. Shadows deepened along a boulevard that once glowed with neon lights, streetlamps, and passing traffic. The great slab of the high-rise hotel was a dark tombstone set against the red sky of a setting sun.

As Levon closed on the place, he saw fresh bullet holes in every surface. Pockmarks showed where the damage had been repaired following the previous conflicts when coalition forces from America, Britain, and its allies took Mosul. Enduring Freedom overthrew Saddam, and more battles followed with the surge and Sunni uprising. A decade and a half of the war was visible everywhere in the city.

Bazît halted in the middle of the street to look up the face of the building, as though hoping to see his girls looking down at him from one of the terraces above. The longing was visible in the Yazidi's eyes. His usual pirate scowl melted into a mask of naked apprehension.

Levon cleared his throat to break the spell. Bazît's stoic glower returned, the mask once more in place.

"Patience, my friend. If they are here, we will find them," Levon said.

Bazît's head bobbed once in a nod. He clapped a hand to Levon's shoulder.

Levon left Bazît and Hejar behind to move forward alone. He approached the makeshift barrier of earth-filled drums that blocked the road before the hotel. A man with a face ravaged by acne raised a hand for him to stop. Some boys walked over to check out the newcomer. More to break the monotony of the long day than as a threatening gesture.

"*As-salaam'alaykum,*" Levon said. He did not meet the scarred man's eyes. He did not smile.

"*As-salaam'alaykum,*" the scarred man said. An edge of suspicion plain in his voice. "Who are you? Who are you with?"

"I am with the cause, brother. I am with the caliph. I follow the Word and the Law," Levon said.

"That is all so much shit." The scarred man spat a stream that splashed on the asphalt at Levon's feet.

"We are looking for women. We were told you had Yazidi girls here."

"Who told you this?"

"Someone in the souk at Bab al-Toub. His name was Yusef."

"I know a lot of Yusefs."

"This one had white in his beard," Levon said.

The scarred man nodded.

"So, brother. Do you have any Yazidi girls here?" Levon poked a hand into a pocket and came up with a couple of packs of cigarettes. They were still in cellophane and free of tax stamps. Smokes looted from an American PX stockpile.

The scarred man took one pack and tossed the other to the boys who moved closer.

"We have women. But they are ours. None to share," the scarred man said.

"That is not what I heard, brother."

"You are not my brother. You are not Arab."

"I am a brother in the Word of the Prophet."

The scarred man's face creased in a grimace. He spat again, this time to one side, away from Levon.

"You have money?" the scarred man said.

"What I do not have, I can get," Levon said. He patted the pocket the cigarettes had come from.

"You cannot buy a woman here. But you might be able to rent one." The grimace turned to a smile that revealed teeth yellow as dried corn. The younger men grinned and nodded.

"Is what I hear true then? Do you have Yazidi girls?"

"You like them? You like those Shaitan bitches?"

"I hear they are sweet. They have eyes like cats."

"It is eyes that interest you?" the scarred man said. He was enjoying the snickers of the younger men.

"My interests lie lower," Levon said.

The men nodded, grins creasing their faces.

"Your Arabic is good for an Englishman." The scared man's grin shrank. He ran new eyes over Levon's outfit.

"I'm Canadian."

"That is like an American."

"Nothing like an American." Levon spat on the ground.

"You found the prophet there?"

"At a mosque. Akrom Jomaa Madjid in Calgary. I

learned Arabic there. I wanted to read the word in its original form."

"You are a convert." The scarred man's nose wrinkled at the thought at that.

"I am. I wasn't born to Islam."

"Your cock is cut?" The younger guys tittered at that.

"You have girls then?" Levon said. He feigned annoyance.

"None for you." The scarred man turned his back and tossed a pack of Kools to one of the younger men.

Levon rejoined Bazît and Hejar waiting in the shadows of a burned-out restaurant.

"They are here."

41

Carrie woke to someone pounding on the front door. She tried to shake Greg awake. He slapped her hand away with a curse. She shook him harder, and he climbed from the warm bed to head downstairs. The pounding continued on the door. Shouting voices joined the sounds from below.

The house was alight with a shimmering glow coming through the windows from outside. Carrie went to the window. A group of her neighbors, dressed for bed under winter coats, were standing in the driveway, talking and pointing. Their shadows were long on the asphalt, thrown by the same source of light that was illuminating the rooms of the house.

She went to the window at the back of the room and let out a scream.

The garage was on fire. The interior was like a furnace. Black smoke poured up from the open door. More rose from the roof.

She was halfway down the stairs, one foot in a slipper and the other bare, when she remembered the children.

She ran back upstairs and down the hall calling Blaine's name. He only came awake when she pulled the headphones from his head.

Lisa came out into the hall blinking.

"Get the other one and come downstairs. We need to get out of the house," Carrie shouted as she shoved a stumbling Blaine ahead of her for the stairs.

"Merry's not in her bed," Lisa said.

———

Maybe it was the same interrogation room she was in before. Merry couldn't be sure. A state trooper sat across the table from her, along with the grandma-type clerk who'd been so nice to her before. The sharp scent of wood smoke and gasoline came off Merry's clothes.

"Why did you set fire to the garage?" the statie said.

"Aren't you supposed to read me my rights?" Merry said.

"You're a minor. Different rules." The statie was getting impatient.

"That's not true," the clerk said.

The statie sighed and read Merry her rights from a laminated card he'd taken from the breast pocket of his uniform shirt.

"Tell us why you did it, dear," the clerk said. The statie rolled his eyes as he stuffed the card back in place.

Merry told them about Lisa and Blaine. Mrs. Knox locking her in her room. The indifference of the social worker. The threat from Blaine.

The statie cleared his throat. The clerk pressed her lips closed and gave Merry a searching look.

"Excuse us," the clerk said. They left Merry alone in the room.

She sipped the soda the clerk had given her. She was aware that the camera mounted high on the wall was watching.

42

Gunny Leffertz said:

"There's no bottom to what one man will do to another."

There were kids everywhere. Boys, mostly. Boys almost entirely. Children orphaned by the occupation. They wandered the streets in packs. They squatted in ruins. Anyone old enough to carry a rifle was drafted into the cause. Others were used to haul water when the pipes went dry. Or they carried goods and ammo away from places Daesh looted. But most were idle and looking to get in trouble like kids anywhere.

They threw rocks at passing armored vehicles and ran giggling for cover as answering fire tore the air above them. They begged for food or cigarettes in the streets. That brought them kicks or fists. They got up out of the dust and returned to pleading from any passing vehicle or pedestrian.

Levon saw a boy he guessed was no older than eight standing at a corner with a hand out and calling praise for Allah. His other hand gripped the wrist of a little girl who looked to be three. A bag tossed from a passing truck tumbled to the street. The boy released the hand of the toddler to shove hunks of bread from the bag into his mouth. The little girl reached for the bag. The boy slapped her hand away. She persisted, and he shoved her hard to the curb. She stood mutely watching, eyes longing, as he finished every crumb of the bread. He then took her hand once more and continued begging from any who passed.

The three men were followed by a loose column of children as they walked the streets around the hotel.

"These kids are trouble," Levon said to Bazît.

"They see everything. They are like watchdogs," Bazît said.

"Maybe they can be watchdogs for us," Levon said.

Hejar, walking ahead, came to a stop before an apartment block. It was a ten-story tower that would look more at home in Belgium. A corner of the building from the sixth floor down had collapsed recently. Either a direct hit from an air strike or some structural flaw exposed by the tremors caused by high explosive ordnance dropped in the near vicinity.

"Looks good," Levon said. He leaned back to look up the scorched face of the building. It was probably a high-end residence at one time. Home to doctors or business owners. Now it was a ruin.

"Looks to me like it wants to fall down," Bazît said. His frown deepened.

"The roof will give us a vantage point of the Azur. And it looks like we'll be the only tenant," Levon said.

"With good reason," Bazît said.

Hejar had already gone inside the dark lobby. He returned and waved them forward. The straggling band of kids followed. Bazît waved them away. He kicked bits of rubble at them. Most ran off. Two remained, watching the men in silence.

"There is a stairwell that is clear," Hejar said.

"All the way to the top?" Levon said.

"I could not see. Perhaps."

With Hejar leading the way they climbed the dark stairwell from landing to landing. Shafts of sunlight lanced through the dark from holes punched in the structure made by shrapnel. The wind made a high-pitched fluting sound through the gaps. Levon could feel the steps sway beneath his boots. Below them, the two boys followed. They kept two floors between them and the three strange men climbing above. They were trying to move quietly. It was impossible on the debris-strewn steps. The snap of crushed glass and scrape of concrete echoed up the tower.

"We should kill them," Bazît said.

"We probably should. But we're not going to," Levon said.

Bazît hawked and spat a stream down the stairwell. His temper was shorter now. He was closer to his daughters and fighting to tame his impatience. Without Levon's influence, he would have charged into the Azur, killing all who stood between him and the girls, and damn the consequences. But his friend advised caution. They must have a plan, a strategy, if Bazît was to find his girls and bring them out of Mosul safely.

The roof was a flat expanse surrounded by a chest-high curtain wall of concrete block. The only feature standing above the roof line was a cluster of satellite dishes arrayed along one side. There was a jagged stress crack running across the damaged corner of the building. They dropped their gear in the corner opposite. Levon took a peek over the wall. The Plaza Azur stood on the next block over. The entrance of the hotel was hidden by lower buildings standing between. But the floors from three up were clearly visible along the hotel's western and southern faces.

Levon scanned the windows with a 30x scope. The glass that remained glowed in the lowering sun with a golden glare. He handed the scope off to Bazît.

"Farhad's wife, Dersima, said your girls are on the seventh floor," Levon said.

Bazît played the lens over the face of the hotel.

Hejar crunched toward them over the roof. In each hand, he held a boy by the collar. The boys dangled as they walked, toes dancing over the gravel surface. Their arms and legs were stick-thin. When they got closer, Levon could see the signs of malnourishment. Their flesh was shrunken, giving their faces a skull-like appearance. They had the eyes of old men. The oldest was maybe nine. His companion a year or so younger. There was no fear as Hejar hoisted them up to the wall and tilted his head toward the ten-story drop below. Levon gestured for him to let the boys down.

"This is a mistake," Bazît said. He spoke in Kurd so the pair would not understand.

"I will take responsibility," Levon said.

"You will take responsibility, but all of us will die. These two will sell us for a mouthful of rice."

"Then we won't give them anything to sell."

Levon shared some food with them. Bazît and Hejar

strung up a tarp for a hide. The boys ate greedily at first. Levon took the food from them, warning them to eat slowly or risk throwing it up. A can of pears. An MRE of chili with beans scooped up with flaps of bread. A peanut and honey bar. It all vanished into their champing mouths. They sucked crumbs from greasy fingers.

While they ate, they listened. Their eyes strayed to the three strangers speaking in Arabic now. Their ears strained to hear, to learn about these men.

What they heard was a fiction started by Levon and agreed upon by Bazît. All for the ears of the boys. Hejar remained silent. They spoke of their orders from the emir of the Nahawand. They were here on this rooftop to provide cover for traffic along Ninevah Street. It was poor theater and the boys lost interest. The youngest was soon fast asleep, belly full, in the long shadows cast by the curtain wall. The older boy remained awake, squatting on his heels, keeping a keen eye on the strangers.

"They're brothers," Levon said. He nodded toward the boys. One curled up asleep, the other watchful as a sentry dog.

"They are trouble," Bazît said under his breath.

43

Nancy Valdez was trying hard to keep her growing impatience out of her voice.

"You do have a Meredith Cade in your system?" she said.

"I can confirm that. I cannot tell you any more than that." The woman on the other end of the phone was covering her own irritation with a blanket of Southern charm. She was the public defender assigned to Merry Cade on the arson charges.

"You understand that this girl is a material witness in a major federal investigation?"

"I do understand. But *you* understand that, as a juvenile, the child's records are sealed."

"Even in an open case?"

"*Especially* in an open case."

"You see, I need access to the Cade girl. Her father is a federal fugitive and I need her monitored for any contact she might have with him."

"Is she in danger from him?"

Nancy wasn't sure how to answer that. She decided to play on the woman's sympathies.

"Levon Cade is a serial murderer who abducted his daughter following the murder of her maternal grandparents. They had legal guardianship of her." It was half truth, and half lie. Let Daisy Mae work it out on her own.

"That's terrible. That poor girl."

"You see why I need to know her current location," Nancy said.

"But, as I already told you, I'm not at liberty to share that information."

"Is there another way around this? I need to maintain contact. Help me out here."

"I can give you the number of her GAL."

"Gal? Her *gal*?"

"That's her *Guardian Ad Litem*. A juvenile advocate assigned to Meredith by the court. She might be able to help you but I'm betting she'll only tell you the same thing I just did."

"Can you give me her number?" Nancy said. She heard fingers tapping a keyboard on the other end.

"Her name is Betsy Ritter. I have her cell here."

———

They called it a youth study center. Merry knew it was really a jail. They gave her a room to herself for the first few nights. Just a bed and wall shelf for her belongings. A personal hygiene pack with soap, toothbrush and paste, and comb. And a change of clothes and underwear. The windows didn't open but the door was unlocked. The bathroom was shared with the other girls on this floor.

There was a television room at the end of the hall, and the television was on all the time during daylight hours. Adding to the noise from the TV were the voices of other girls talking, laughing, and arguing.

Merry stayed to herself except for when the matrons took them down to a dining room, where they were fed meals prepared for them somewhere else. The facility didn't have a kitchen. The food was like the meals she used to get at elementary school. Cereal and a banana for breakfast. A sandwich and apple at lunch. A meat and veggie or spaghetti at dinner with a piece of vanilla cake or pudding cup. All served in foam clamshells with plastic forks and knives.

The only difference between the YSC and Calhoun Middle was it being girls only. Merry sat alone to eat, ignored by the others. And it was boring. The view from her window was a parking lot. There was nothing to read but old magazines like *People* or *Us*. The television room wasn't inviting. Girls talking in competition with the volume of radios turned to maximum. Sometimes she could hear them arguing over the remote in English and Spanish.

Her only welcome distraction was two visits from a new woman assigned to her from Child Services.

Betsy Ritter was as different from Miss Nussbaum as it was possible to be. She wasn't much taller than Merry. A ninety-pound ball of energy fueled by Starbucks and two packs of Kools a day. She had a shock of white-blonde hair that looked like she combed it with her fingers once a day. And she didn't dress like Miss Nussbaum. A black concert T-shirt of bands Merry never heard of, jeans, and sneakers.

The second time they met was in a small conference

room on the first floor. Betsy brought Wendy's burgers and Cokes that they shared. Merry had told her Wendy's was her favorite when Betsy asked at the close of their first meeting.

She also told Betsy everything that happened in the Knox house and Miss Nussbaum's failure to act to protect her and Lisa.

"I'm going to do what I can to keep you in a single room," Betsy said.

"Thank you."

"I don't think you'll be here very long. A few more nights."

"Okay."

"They have you over to the courthouse for a hearing on Monday, but I think charges will be dropped against you. This Blaine character is being held on statutory. Dumb son of a bitch had his eighteenth birthday last month so he's over in county. Believe me; he's having a worse time than you. Basically, the whole thing is a big fat embarrassment to the whole county."

"How is Lisa?"

"She's in a new home. They've assigned her to me. I can vouch for these new folks. I've placed kids there before."

"Are the Knoxes mad about their garage?"

"To hell with them, okay? They should never have been fostering anyone with that sick bastard of a son in the house. You have nothing to be sorry for, you hear?"

"I guess."

"Tell me about what family you have. How did you wind up in foster care?"

Merry told her story, as much of it as she felt anyone outside of her and her father needed to know. Betsy took notes in a thick leather-bound pad bristling with Post-its. Betsy interrupted now and then with a question.

"And you have no idea where your father is?"

"No, ma'am."

"You wouldn't be telling me a story?"

"No, ma'am. I don't know where my daddy is."

"And your uncle is the only other family you have?"

"There's more relatives up in Tennessee. I have an uncle Wendell in Murfreesboro but I never met him."

"Is Wendell's last name Cade too?"

"I think so. He's Uncle Fern's cousin."

Betsy wrote the name down in her book.

"I'll contact them and your Uncle Fern. We'll see if the court will let them have custody of you. Anything else, Merry?"

"Did you find out about the books I borrowed from Ms. Booth? They were her personal books. I don't want her to think I kept them."

"I called her like you asked me. She understands. They were just paperbacks."

"I wish I had them here. There's nothing to read."

"Shit. I almost forgot." Betsy dug into the canvas boat bag that looked like it weighed half as much as she did. She came up with a pair of digest-sized magazines and handed them over.

Merry took them eagerly. Two copies of something called *Ellery Queen's Mystery Magazine*. One featured an illustration of a police officer kneeling to read the pulse of a young girl lying dead on a sidewalk. The other had a woman pulling a gun from a desk drawer as a shadowy figure loomed close.

"You said you liked mysteries, right? My mom has *boxes* of these in the garage."

"These are great!" Merry was already flipping through them.

"I'll bring more next time. It won't be until the day after tomorrow. But you'll be okay, right?"

The GAL left Merry already engrossed in a story.

Out on the parking lot, the cell in Betsy's bag began buzzing from somewhere inside her voluminous bag. A ringtone of The Pixies' "Debaser." She set the bag on the hood of her Golf and dug the phone out—a two-zero-two number on the screen.

"Ritter here."

The caller introduced herself as Nancy Valdez, Department of Treasury.

"How can I help you, Agent Valdez?"

Betsy leaned back on her eight-year-old V-dub, smoked a Kool, and listened until Agent Valdez finished her story.

"Well, I hate to ruin your day, honey," Betsy said.

But she went ahead and did it anyway.

"There's this girl's privacy issues. She's a minor in custody of the county. Before that, she was a ward of the county," Betsy said.

"You understand that this is a federal criminal case and possible matter of national security. I need access to Meredith Cade in order to both protect her, and apprehend her father." This chick was all business.

"Is that why you had her placed in that sick-ass house? To *protect* her?"

"I had no control over where she was placed."

"That's not what I heard, honey." The 'honey' was the sting in the tail.

"What are you implying?"

"I'm implying shit. I asked around the courthouse and

there was some outside pressure to get the girl placed in the first available slot. By doing that, you placed her in danger. And I'm guessing a whole hell of a lot more danger than her father represents to her."

The voice from Washington turned steely. "I'll get access with or without your help."

"I'm sure you will. But you're going to do it the hard way. Meredith is in Alabama now. You need to start at county level and find a judge to sign off on it. I hope you know what you're up against there."

"We'll go through due process, believe me. We only want what's in the best interest of the child."

"Well, bless your heart," Betsy said and broke the connection.

Maybe the bitch on the other end of the phone knew it or maybe she didn't. But "bless your heart" in this instance was pure Dixie for "go fuck yourself."

44

As the daylight died, the wind shifted westerly, bringing with it the stink of the diesel fires burning to the east. It settled in the streets in a greasy funk. The last call to pray of the day brought a quiet across the city. Only the thump of distant artillery strikes could be heard against the breathless silence that cloaked the city while the invaders took to their prayer mats in robotic supplication. The heavy traffic of shells sounded like the rumble of surf from an invisible sea.

Prayers over, the sounds of Mosul returned. Radios played the overlapping scolds of imams and emirs and, here and there, snatches of music. And all punctuated by sounds of gunfire, as natural now as the calls of birds.

Levon watched through the night. His right eye pressed to the cup of the 30x, he swept the hotel with his left in search of movement. The powerful lens brought the windows and balconies of the Azur close enough to touch. Men stepped out on the balconies to smoke and catch the night breeze. Their conversations echoed over the rooftops. The words were unintelligible, but Levon knew the rhythm. The ball-busting and bullshitting of rough men awaiting action. It would be louder if they were allowed alcohol.

He looked for glimpses of light coming through from parted curtains as men moved in and out of the rooms. He kept a special concentration on the seventh floor. Brief glimpses showed him room interiors like any other hotel anywhere else in the world. Some of the windows glowed with the pulsing blue nimbus of light cast by television screens.

Hours into his watch, he swung the scope to a sudden spark of yellow light. A man was silhouetted as he parted a curtain to step out onto the balcony. The man halted a moment, holding the gap open. Maybe speaking to someone inside or holding the curtain open for another to follow. Levon focused through the narrow triangle of light and into the room beyond.

A female figure sat at a table inside, her back to Levon's view. She wore a black hijab that hid the shape of her head. To his eye she looked petite when scaled against the height of the table. The curtain dropped closed, the slice of light vanishing. In the half second before the balcony went dark the girl at the table turned her head. She was young. She was speaking to someone deeper in the room and out of sight. Her nose was thin with a tiny turn at the end. Her eyes were cast down so that he could not have seen their color even if the distance allowed it.

Through the scope he swept down the building, counting the floors as he went. The girl was on the seventh floor. He couldn't be certain of the girl's identity. He'd only seen Bazît's daughters in a photo that was years old. The girl he saw might be a Yazidi. If he could only see her eyes, he'd be certain.

Levon stayed in place, the scope trained on the window where he'd seen the girl. The room behind the drapes went dark. He kept watch.

The moon dropped below the urban horizon. A movement behind the glass of the window. Blue shadows shifted, a flash of silver. A figure stepped onto the balcony. A small figure. It stepped forward to the curtain wall, leaning over the top to drop something that fluttered down to the street.

The focus sharpened to fix on a young girl, her head uncovered. Hair the color of wheat. She was stretching over the top of the balcony wall to release bits of paper. The paper was white and fell like petals to the street. She watched the shreds drifting away down the face of the building. She then dropped back onto the balcony.

For less than a second, she gazed in Levon's direction. Her eyes were the color of the desert at twilight.

Just like her father's.

The sky glowed a shimmering electric blue along the peaks to the east as dawn neared.

———

Three jets banked high in a cloudless morning sky. They roared overhead at intervals, invisible but for silver flashes off their wings at six thousand feet. The anti-aircraft fire pumped at them was purely symbolic. White flashes arced upward only to arrive too late and fall too short of offering any threat to the fast-moving jets. Across the city, small arms fire erupted in pops and stutters. Rifles fired either in impotent rage or to break the tedium.

Black specks tumbled down in the wake of the aircraft already thirty miles away and climbing on a triple sonic boom. The specks took on the shapes of lozenges just before dropping out of sight behind buildings. Great yellow-brown clouds blossomed where the JDAMs came to their final rest.

The roof of the apartment building shuddered even though the line of blasts was exploding more than four miles to the north. Hejar awoke with a start, bits of gravel dancing across the rooftop as the earth shook under him. He'd fallen asleep the night before while keeping a watchful eye on the two orphan boys. The pair of them slept through the tremor. One of them raised filthy fingers to scratch an itch on his neck.

Across the roof, Bazît dozed against the curtain wall. Next to him, Levon lay on a tabletop they'd dragged up to the roof the night before. It was set so the flat surface was almost level with the curtain wall. It was covered over with the tarp to provide shade and to conceal whoever lay there. Levon had his 30x in his hands and kept a close watch on the two faces of the French hotel visible to them across the other side of the block.

The call to prayer rose in a tinny voice from a hundred loudspeakers mounted on the towers of a dozen mosques. One *adhan* began seconds behind another, until all was a rising and falling electronic buzz punctuated by piercing shrieks of feedback.

Hejar washed his face with a handful of bottled water. His eyes were crusty, and his mouth was dry. He finished the water and crushed the bottle before tossing it aside. He walked to Levon's side. The American had a scrap of paper by him weighted down with a chunk of concrete. He'd written on it in marker.

"What is this?" Hejar said.

"It's a timeline. There was a rolling blackout last night. I checked the time and length. It might be a pattern," Levon said.

"You were awake all night?"

"Most of it."

Hejar thought back. He could not recall ever seeing the American asleep. Levon rolled off the tabletop and crouched by the nodding Bazît.

"What kind of pattern?" Hejar said.

"One section of the city goes dark for an hour or two. And then another. I could see it from here. It looked like a planned outage."

"How does this help us?" Bazît said.

"The Azur's power went off just before oh-two-hundred. There was a ninety-second lag until the generators kicked on. That's our window." Levon snapped the top off a water bottle. He took a long pull on it, recapped it, and tossed it to one of the boys. They were awake now and watching the men with interest. The two boys shared the bottle until it was dry.

"I grow impatient," Bazît said.

"I agree. We can position ourselves tonight to move when the power goes dark," Levon said.

"A ninety-second window. Is it enough?"

"We could extend it." Levon looked to Hejar who appeared puzzled.

"You will make certain the generator does not start," Bazît said.

Hejar nodded.

"Can you do it quietly?" Levon said.

Hejar grinned. The first time Levon had seen him smile. It was not a pretty sight.

"Where is the generator?" Bazît said.

"Not sure. Somewhere out of sight. I heard it come on just before the lights. It's a big one. Big enough to power up most of the hotel lights. It's probably in the courtyard behind the building," Levon said.

"We must be sure," Bazît said.

"We will be," Levon said. His eyes were on the pair of boys peeling open an MRE they found lying by his pack.

45

"You are not Arab," Yasin said. He was the older of the two brothers. The youngest was Zamir.

"I'm Canadian," Levon lied. "I was born with the name Jonathan. But I am Rohan Haddad now."

"You come to be Daesh?" Yasin said.

"Yes. I believe in the caliphate. I believe it is God's will that this land returns to Sharia."

Yasin turned to blink into the sun. His brother sat on the gravel in the shade of the curtain wall, watching birds fluttering down to roost on the forest of satellite dishes. He threw a piece of gravel that clanged off a dish. It sent the birds flying.

"Daesh killed my parents." Yasin said it as plain fact. There was no rancor or remorse in his voice.

"It was God's will," Levon said.

Yasin wrinkled his nose at that.

"You have good food," the boy said.

"It is yours to share," Levon said.

"And what must we do for it?"

The price. Everything came down to a price.

"I need you to tell me where something is."

"What?"

"A machine. A generator. It's somewhere out of sight where I can't see it."

"Behind the building you watch."

"Yes. Behind the Hotel Azur."

Yasin looked to Levon's pack. He ran a tongue over his teeth.

"All you want," Levon said.

"Why does Daesh watch Daesh?"

"Do you care?"

Yasin studied Levon's face a moment.

"No," the boy said.

He stepped over to his brother and took the younger boy's hand. He lifted Zamir to his feet. Together they walked to the shed where the stairwell exited. They entered to start the long descent down to the street.

"And what makes you believe those two will not turn us in at the first opportunity?" Bazît said.

"We fed them," Levon said.

"The Sunnis might feed them too." Bazît shook his head and kicked at the gravel.

"You see those kids? Living worse than stray dogs. All they can think of is filling their bellies."

"Dogs bite their masters, too." Bazît turned to walk to the corner of the rooftop. He leaned over the curtain wall and watched the two brothers pick their way over the broken concrete that lay in the alley below. They navigated between tangles of rusting rebar toward the tower of the French hotel.

"Hejar. You better follow them," Levon said.

Hejar rolled from under the awning and picked up his rifle to trot to the stairwell.

———

Levon walked down to street level while Bazît kept watch from the hide. He climbed over rubble and down narrow alleys to a broader avenue that intersected Nineveh Street. He walked a few blocks south, along with people heading back and forth to the local market. The women were covered head to toe in dark cloth, eyes cast to the road as they carried bags loaded with goods. The men walked casually, talking with companions. An imam led a gaggle of silent schoolboys toward a mosque. The voices of clerics murmured from radios all along the roadway.

He bought a bottle of water from a street vendor. He turned the cap, listening to the crack of plastic, before paying. It was a new bottle. The vendor nodded and grinned. Water purification in Mosul was as spotty as the electric service. The water coming from the taps was loaded with bacteria and rust.

Traffic on the street was confined to up-armored pickup trucks, packed with glowering men armed to the teeth. ISIS was rich in oil, but poor in fuel. There were no refineries in the regions they controlled. While they found ready buyers for their crude on the world spot market, actual gasoline and diesel were hard to come by. Rationing was strict about keeping the jihadi vehicles active and the power plant running.

He needed a ride. One that would provide natural camouflage. Any pickups, Toyotas, and Hyundais he saw parked were all set at intersections and fully manned. Young men lounged around them, smoking and bullshitting. A mile along the avenue brought him to a pocket park. It was empty of all but a few old men talking quietly around a bone-dry fountain at the center of the open lot.

In the corner of the lot, a young man worked under the hood of a pickup pulled up in the shade of some cedars. An Isuzu pickup painted in a dappled improvised camouflage pattern. It sagged under the weight of an anti-aircraft gun bolted down in the bed. A limp black ISIS flag swayed on a pole behind the cab. The young man was squatting over an open toolbox and cursing under his breath when Levon walked up to him.

"That model is temperamental," Levon said.

The young man glanced up at the tall stranger. His eyes narrowed and his mouth turned down.

"Your Arabic is good. Where does a white man learn to speak like this?"

"I married an Egyptian girl."

The young man shrugged.

Levon leaned his rifle against a fender and bent to look under the hood of the truck. The engine block was coated with the gummy residue of old grease from a bad seal.

"It won't start?"

"It is a bitch!" The young man tossed a wrench that bounced off the grill.

"My brother had one of these back in Derry."

"Derry?"

"In Ireland. I'd never miss a chance to kill Englishmen."

The young man's suspicion melted into a grin.

"I heard that the Irish like to fight," he said.

"You heard right, my friend. Especially when the fight is a righteous one."

"Allahu akbar," the young man said, ducking his head.

"Allahu akbar," Levon said. "Now what's the trouble with this bitch?"

"It will not start."

"Give it a try."

The young man got in the cab and turned the key. An anemic clicking and tapping died away to a sputter, then silence. The battery was good. Levon went to the toolbox for a crescent wrench to loosen the belts and pull the alternator. The young man watched as the stranger took the alternator apart with expert ease and laid the pieces on a greasy towel on the ground.

"Diode looks okay. A lot of carbon. You're not getting much of a spark," Levon said. He pointed to the disassembled barrel shape—rings, bearings, fan, and plates. The young man nodded in mute agreement.

Levon cleaned the brushes and slip ring and reassembled the alternator. With the young man's help he replaced it under the Isuzu's hood and adjusted the belt tension. Leads in place, he stepped back and told the young man to give it another go. After a rattle, the truck roared to life. The young man's face split into a grin.

"You're going to need to replace the unit. But you're good for a while. As long as it's running, anyway," Levon said. He replaced the tools in the box and wiped his hands on the towel.

"My brothers will be pleased. They did not believe I could get it working again," the young man called over the rumbling engine. He cut the power and stepped from the cab to stand before the truck.

"Where are your brothers?" Levon asked.

The old men shuffled away from the fountain. The park was empty.

"They went to the market, left me here to work on

the truck. I am good with motors." The young man shut the hood and stepped back toward Levon.

"Do you have a car you dream of owning one day?" Levon said from behind him.

The boy was picturing a silver Mercedes when his new friend's arm snaked around his neck. With his free hand Levon gripped his fist and pressed it toward him. The boy's throat was trapped in the crook of Levon's arm. He bucked against the pressure, kicking at the ground and clawing at Levon's sleeve. His hands fell away, his legs trembled. A stream of piss spilled over his feet making a puddle in the dust. Levon kept the pressure on even after the body went slack.

He dropped the young man to the ground. His windpipe crushed and his brain starved of blood. The boy's eyes were crimson from broken vessels. His mouth was bloody where he'd bitten through his tongue.

Levon dumped the body into the bed of the Isuzu by the base of the AAA gun. He covered it over with the ISIS flag torn from the pole. Behind the wheel, he cranked the engine to life once more. He dropped it into gear and pulled from under the trees and onto the street. He drove away from the market for a few blocks. After two right turns he pointed the truck back toward the apartment block where Bazît waited.

46

He found Yasin and Zamir asleep in the shade at the top of the stairs. The litter of three MREs lay torn open and licked clean by them. Their mouths were greasy rings. Levon stepped over them onto the rooftop. A sack bulging with more goodies was hugged in the arms of the older brother. The drawstring looped around Yasin's reed-thin wrist.

"They did as you asked them," Hejar said.

Bazît showed Levon a crude drawing made in marker on a piece of cardboard torn from a carton. It showed the rectangle of the Azur and lines representing a privacy fence that surrounded a courtyard behind the hotel. The pool was shown as an oval.

"What's this?" Levon said. He pointed at some squiggles in the corner of the courtyard.

"The generator. They said it is under an awning against the rear of the building," Bazît said.

"The boys said there were many Daesh around the pool. They were roasting a sheep. I could smell it," Hejar said.

"They should be gone by night," Levon said.

"Unless they sleep outside," Bazît said.

"Not with the nights getting colder," Hejar said.

"Did they see any women? Girls?" Levon said.

Hejar shook his head.

"We go tonight?" Bazît said.

"Tonight," Levon said.

———

"Those boys are gone." Bazît was touching his arm. "They have left."

Levon came awake. It was late afternoon when he'd closed his eyes for a moment. The sky was gray now.

"When?"

"I did not see them leave. I was watching the hotel."

"Hejar?"

"He was down getting the truck ready."

Levon stood to look out over the city. Lights were coming on. A spray of tracers flew upward from somewhere. The boom of a passing jet invisible in the gloom above.

"Did they take anything?" Levon lifted a rucksack to spill its contents onto the roof. His backpack, with the bundle of cash, lay under him while he was sleeping.

"Maybe." Bazît shrugged.

"There's not as much as there was earlier. They took all the MREs and cigarettes."

"They will betray us."

"More likely? They saw us running low on stuff and decided to grab what they could and run. Just hungry kids."

"I would feel better if they were dead. You would not listen."

"Those boys are just a little bit younger than your daughters."

"They are Sunni. They will be Daesh. They will serve whoever feeds them. From cubs come wolves."

"I'm not saying you're wrong."

"Have you had to kill a child, Levon Cade?"

"Someone told me that I'm a kind man but not a good man."

Bazît's eyes narrowed.

A low whistle from the stairwell. Hejar was returning.

"It will be full dark in two hours. That's when we move. A little over four hours until the rolling blackout hits." Levon picked up his rifle and moved to the tarp-covered hide.

47

"Hello. Fern here."

"Uncle Fern?"

"That you, Merry girl?"

"It's me."

"Damn, it's good to hear your voice. I've been missing having you around here."

"I miss you too. And the farm."

"Don't worry yourself about the farm. I'm taking good care of your pony. Dr. Jessie's been by to check on him. Says he's healthy as a horse. Well, that just makes sense, doesn't it?"

"And the goat?"

"The goat's just fine. Goats are tough as leather."

"That's good."

"They going to let you come home soon, Merry?"

"I don't know. A nice lady here says I'll be going with family somewhere. Either with you or in Tennessee."

"Wendell and Alma. But you've never even met them, have you?"

"Nope. I never even *heard* of them before I met you.

And I thought you were somebody my daddy made up for the stories he told me."

"They treating you okay, honey?"

"They are now. What about you? You still in trouble?"

"Well, they tore the place up pretty good looking for something. Had cops from all over stomping through here, ripping up the barn floor. They even dug a few holes and found nothing. But they've been leaving me alone the last few days."

"I'm so sorry, Uncle Fern."

"No need for that. I've always been in trouble of one kind or another."

"They're telling me my time is up. I have to go."

"You take care, honey."

"See you soon, Uncle Fern."

Nancy Valdez tore headphones from her head and threw them to the console. Chad Bengstrom snatched up a canned soda before it spilled onto his keyboard.

"Not one goddamned word about her father!" she said. She shoved away from the desk.

"And nothing about her location," Laura Strand said.

"That bitch social worker has her hidden away in the system down there. I'm having to deal with county judges and getting nowhere. They think the Civil War is still going on." Nancy paced the quad like a caged animal.

"Anything else on the hillbilly's phone?" Tony Marcoon said around a wad of nicotine gum.

"The guy never talks to anyone," Chad said.

"This is the first call he's had all week," Laura said.

"Ed Bowden called it 'mountain pride,'" Tony said.

"Just another way of saying criminal conspiracy," Nancy said. "They're waiting us out. Hoping the investigation ends so Cade can resurface and cash in."

"Or they really *don't* know where he is, or anything about this pile of cash we're theorizing about," Laura said.

"We stay up on the tap. See where the daughter lands. Work another angle then," Nancy said.

48

Gunny Leffertz said:

"When you're fucked, you're fucked. No use crying. All you can do is get yourself un-fucked."

The temperatures dropped to near freezing. The air was damp, making for a bone-chilling cold. The miserable weather enforced the curfew with more authority than the truckloads of gunmen cruising the streets watching for offenders.

Somewhere along the river, a series of explosions created a sudden and brief corona along the horizon that threw the skyline to the east into a stark eclipse. Responding AAA fire lanced into the sky, seeking targets in a reverse meteor shower. Small arms erupted in accompaniment, red streaks arcing into the dark in impotent fury.

The sentries before the Hotel Azur were down to a

skeleton crew. All of the idle loafers who were out on the street all afternoon were warm inside now. The power was still up on this block, slits of yellow glow in the gaps of blackout curtains. The shimmering aquatic light of television screens.

Levon and Bazit crouched in the dark of a shuttered shop across the boulevard from the hotel front. They'd entered the store from the alley in the rear an hour before. The place was a bakery of some kind and showed signs of looting. Smashed display cases left a carpet of broken glass on the floor that crunched underfoot. Between the slats of wood covering the windows, Levon watched the hotel front. Three men bundled in hooded coats were standing in the shelter of the canopy above the doors to the main lobby. They were armed but not watchful. Two of them were engaged in conversation. The third appeared to be engrossed in texting on a smartphone.

Twenty minutes until the scheduled blackout.

———

The alley behind the hotel was choked with rubbish, making quiet passage difficult.

Hejar placed his feet carefully between cartons, cans, bottles, and discarded pool furniture to move around to the rear of the building. The wall running about the pool courtyard was a screen of decorative cement block with perforations in a diamond pattern. The opposite side of the alley was a high concrete wall topped with strings of razor wire. A multi-storied car park beyond it.

He was able to see through the design of the wall surrounding the pool to the fully lit courtyard area. He was well concealed in the shadows of the narrow alleyway and could watch unseen. Flickering fluorescents lit the back of the hotel like a stage.

The remains of the sheep roast were still in evidence. The two boys had not lied about that. A stripped rib cage still hung from a spit over a steel tub scorched black. Some café tables and chairs were arranged in a corner piled with paper trash.

The water level in the pool was several feet lower than the tiled rim. Even in the cold air, the stink from the dark water was stomach-turning. Hejar pinched his nostrils closed. He moved along the wall, peering through the holes in the blocks in search of something that looked like a generator. A sort of painted metal cabinet was against a latticework wall. It looked to be ten feet long and three feet high. There were vents and hatches in the steel casing. At the far end was a vertical pipe of PVC with a cap of some sort atop it. He could see cables and pipes running from it and back through the lattice wall. It sat under an awning as the two boys had described.

He crouched in the trash to wait for the lights to die. He slung his rifle across his back. He wiped sweating hands on his pants. From the pocket of his coat, he removed a plastic bag of sand Levon had given him. The American instructed him to find the fuel intake on the generator and pour the sand inside. The generator would fail to start in a way that could be blamed on mechanical problems. It would buy Levon and Bazît a few minutes more time to work their way inside.

No one was out in the courtyard. Shadows moved now and again across the glass of the entrance, but no one came outside. There were no guards in sight. Why would there be? Daesh owned the city. There was no one left to raise a fist to them.

Hejar set the sand sack down and blew warm air into his cupped hands. The sweat left him with a chill. He wished he was with Bazît. He wanted to be with him inside the hotel. Hejar wanted to kill Daesh. It was all he could think of. He had no home, no family. Nothing to go back to but hollow grief and empty graves. This night, deep in the heart of the enemy's stronghold, was a night he had thought of, imagined, ever since ISIS arrived in Sinjar. To send Sunni bastards to hell with bullet and blade became his sole driving purpose. Barely twenty years old, Hejar could not imagine a life past this night. His future had died with his family.

The sudden dark left him blind for a few seconds. All ambient noise from within the hotel died to silence. He had not noticed the sounds until they were absent, the hum of fluorescents and muffled music. Hejar blinked hard once, twice. He felt the ground beneath him for the plastic bag of sand. He placed it between his teeth and climbed the concrete wall.

He dropped to the other side into a crouch and moved low, stepping cautiously. His fear was that he might stumble into the pool, into that reeking pit. It was a mortal fear as Hejar, born of the desert, could not swim. He would sink into the freezing murk to join the rest of the dead lying at the bottom of the pool. He skirted the pool, his vision becoming adjusted to the gloom. A hand brushed the rough wall of the hotel, guiding him toward the generator.

In his mind, he counted off the seconds as he ran hands over the cold metal surface in search of the stand-pipe he spotted earlier. He had ninety seconds, one minute and a half before the generator kicked on. In his mind he counted off the seconds.

Twenty-eight seconds.

His fingers found the cap atop the intake.

Thirty-four seconds.

It refused to turn at first. He gripped it until his fingers and palm hurt. With a whispered curse, he realized he was turning it the wrong way.

Forty seconds.

He shifted his grip and rotated the cap counterclockwise. It gave easily and came away. It went into a pocket of his coat as Levon instructed.

Forty-five seconds.

A sharp chemical smell rose from the open pipe. Hejar opened the plastic sack of sand and, using his hand as a makeshift funnel, poured the contents down the pipe. Taking care, he made sure the bag was empty, every grain down inside the fuel tank.

Fifty-two seconds.

He stuffed the empty bag in a pocket and retrieved the cap. He twisted the cap back in place, fumbling on the first two tries to get the threads lined up right. Levon insisted that the cap had to be put back in place. When the generator did not start up someone would come out to inspect it. If everything were as they expected it to be they would believe that some mechanical problems were causing the motor to be stalled. They would not suspect sabotage.

Sixty-seven seconds.

Hejar's vision had attuned to the dark by now. He moved at a trot for the wall, skirting the edge of the pool easily.

Seventy-five seconds.

Using a café table for a boost, he threw his belly over the top of the wall. He levered himself around and dropped easily into the dark alley.

Eighty-four seconds.

He made his way back along the alley toward the boulevard. His part of the mission now was to get to the truck and wait for his uncle and the American to come to him with Bazît's daughters. A stuttering cough sounded behind him that settled into a regular thumping sound.

Fingers of light appeared in the alley around him, projected through the diamond pattern of the block wall. The lights inside and outside the hotel were coming back on.

He waited, breath held, for the generator to die.

It did not. Its heart beat regular and strong, somewhere out of sight beyond the wall.

From within the hotel, a rash of automatic fire erupted and built to thunder.

49

Gunny Leffertz said:

"When you're making your plans, have a plan for when your plan goes to shit, and then a plan for when that plan goes to shit. Because it will go to shit."

Levon waited, eyes closed. He listened to the street outside. His ears found music playing somewhere, the rhythmic beat of Sufi drums, muted from an apartment somewhere. When the music died to sudden silence, he opened his eyes.

The Hotel Azur and surrounding streets were dark.

Bazît beside him, he stepped from the bakery and crossed the boulevard at a fast walk. They approached the front of the hotel at an angle. Coming up on the three sentries from a blind spot.

Levon stepped to the pair who had been talking earlier. He drew within reach before they knew anything. One after the other, he jammed the Browning into their abdomens for a double tap. Their heavy clothing muffled the blasts. Bazît had done the same to the man with the phone. The report of his revolver was louder than the automatic.

"Take his phone," Levon said. Bazît stooped to pocket it while Levon shouldered his way into the darkness of the hotel lobby. The Yazidi stepped over the bodies of the dead men. No time to conceal them. Every second counted now.

The two men crossed the lobby at a walk. Faint moonlight fell in long purple bars over the furniture and registration desk. There were others here. Shadows only. Muttered voices. No one turned to them or spoke to them as they moved to the stairwell door at the rear of the lobby by the most direct route.

The inside of the stairwell was lightless.

"The phone," Levon said. He felt it placed in his hand and touched the power tab. Holding the screen light before him, Levon led the way up the stairs.

They moved at a run. Bazît was breathing hard after the third landing, grunting to keep up. Levon beat him to the door that exited onto the seventh floor. It was marked with a 'six.' Europeans didn't begin numbering until the second floor.

Levon waited until Bazît, gasping, caught up. Levon tabbed the phone off and pocketed it. He put a shoulder to the door and popped the handle. They stepped into a hallway dimly lit with a glow from windows at either end.

The air smelled of cooking grease and hashish. There were men moving in the hall a few doors down. The red glow of two cigarettes made them known.

Their mumbled conversation was the only sound. Levon and Bazît moved in their direction, toward the place where the hall ended in a "T" intersection. The cross corridor was where they'd find the rooms that lined the southern wall, and the place where Levon saw the girl with the desert twilight eyes. They were seconds from that room.

Then the lights came on.

———

Hejar clambered over the wall and dropped back into the fully lit courtyard.

He chased his shadow around the pool, following a motor sound. It was coming from somewhere beyond the machine he believed was the generator. A voice called from a window somewhere above. It rose in volume, calling after him as he hugged the wall to turn a corner toward the running motor.

The generator sat on a concrete pad behind a low hedge in the corner of the courtyard where the wall of the hotel met the decorative screen wall. It chugged away, belching exhaust from a pipe. He searched for the fuel intake and recalled that he had no more sand. The voice behind him continued calling. He sensed movement behind him—a scrape of leather on cement.

Men were coming around the pool. Four men. Only one held a weapon that Hejar could see. A Kalashnikov dangled under the man's arm on a sling made of knotted rope. They were moving at a casual pace, heads turning to search. They responded to the caller above. Gesturing and arguing in impatient streams of Arabic. Their movement became more purposeful under the directions from above. They moved in a loose spearpoint toward the hedge and the generator.

Hejar stood to full height, his rifle to his shoulder and aimed over the hedge top. He fired a stream at the four men. The closest was the armed man who took three rounds across the chest from inside ten feet. The two to his right fell while the third turned to run. A round took him high in the back followed by a second that entered his skull just above the spine. He tumbled into the pool with a splash. As the boom of Hejar's rifle died away, he could hear shouts echoing down toward him from open windows above.

At a loss as to how to stop the incessant heartbeat of the generator, Hejar stepped back toward the screen wall and emptied the rest of his magazine into the body of the motor. Sparks flew and the air filled with the harsh stink of diesel. The damned thing kept on thrumming, sending power to the lights.

Now there were more men in the courtyard. Hejar slapped a fresh magazine into the AK. He heard a window slide open several floors above him. A man leaned out, silhouetted against the night sky. Hejar sent a long burst upward. Bullets punched the concrete below the window, sending out a spray of fine dust. The man disappeared back inside.

The men in the courtyard opened up, using the muzzle flash behind the hedgerow as a target. Hejar rolled away. Chips of flying stucco rained over him. He lay on his belly and fired at the approaching men from under the hedge. A man fell screaming. The others retreated toward the pool.

He felt brass pelting him from above and flipped to his back. The man in the window, or another, was leaning out firing a rifle down at him. From his supine position, Hejar returned fire, blinded by the flash of his own weapon. Either a hot shell casing or a stray spark ignited a pool of diesel spreading across the pad under the generator. Hejar scrambled to his feet and ran for the screen wall, followed by more rounds. The flames around the generator rose up the wall of the hotel in a sudden rush.

Hejar had his belly on the top of the wall and was levering himself over. A round struck his calf as he dropped. He landed hard; his left leg was numb from the knee down. He knew that would not last long. The pain would come. More rounds ripped through the diamond wall in search of him.

On hands and knees, he crawled through the trash-filled alley, the AK thumping on his back as he moved. Behind him, the fire that engulfed the generator blossomed into a tower of flames. The motor sputtered and coughed and died.

The hotel went dark once more but for the blaze spreading across the courtyard on a lake of ignited fuel.

50

Gunny Leffertz said:

"Navy guy told me once that a bad plan is better than no plan. Sometimes even a sailor has something we can all learn from."

The power restored, the hotel came to life again.

Levon stepped down the hallway to the two men. He wore an easy smile, mumbling a greeting in Arabic. They were surprised but not alarmed to see him. They were both unarmed. Wearing man-jams and sandals only. They stood by an open doorway. From inside the room came the canned gunfire of a video game and the sound of men shouting in play.

Levon raised the M4 to his shoulder when he was an arms-length from the pair. The smokers dropped with double taps to the head. The faux gunfire from the room covered the sound.

He stepped over their bodies into the room where four men in underwear were engrossed in a shooter game on a big screen. Their actual weapons lay discarded on the furniture around them, their hands occupied with game controllers. One turned at his entrance, his nose wrinkled at the scent of burned gunpowder.

A six-round burst knocked them all to the floor, where Levon finished them with point-blank taps to skulls and center mass. A hot coppery smell filled the room. A thick splat of blood on the TV screen bathed the room in a mottled red hue.

Behind him, Bazît was braced in the door. The Yazidi's eyes were wild, whites visible around the pupils. The adrenaline was high, cresting. He turned suddenly to look down the hallway. Dropping to a crouch, he fired a long stream from his AK. He rolled away from the door as return fire shredded the door jamb. Rounds came through the walls at an angle, ripping into the carpet and furniture. A haze of plaster dust swirled in the air. Multiple shooters. It wasn't letting up.

Levon rolled over the back of a sofa and charged toward a companion door. He met it shoulder first and the door crashed inward, taking the hinges and a section of the frame with it. Bazît crawled on knees and fingertips and rolled in after him.

The next room was dark and empty. Boots thumped across the ceiling above them. In the room behind them and the hallway outside, men shouted to be heard over the continuing gunfire. Levon pushed a tall wardrobe over. He used it for cover to empty his rifle into the walls in the direction of the outer corridor. The fire out there turned from rolling thunder to the occasional pop. The voices were quieter, though the exchange was still furious.

"They're getting their shit together. We need to get out of this room." Levon headed for the window and tore the drapes and blackout shade aside. He wrenched the sliding door open and stepped out onto the balcony, followed by Bazît. The balcony ran across the face of the building, interrupted only by a section of wrought iron privacy fencing used to separate each room's balcony from the other. He vaulted a fence to the next balcony.

As he and Bazît reached the corner of the building, the lights of the hotel and the street below went dark again.

————

Hejar struggled to his feet and limped at the best speed he could make toward the street at the end of the alley. The cries of men, trapped in the canyon of the surrounding buildings, seemed to come from every-where at once.

A searing heat was building in his calf. Every step brought new pain. He could feel his boot filling with blood, the sock sodden with it.

At the end of the alley he slung the rifle under one arm and forced himself to walk normally. The front of the parking garage and the entire street was dark. He stayed close to the shadows as he moved north along the cross street toward the boulevard. Others, all grown men, moved along the street on one errand or another. No one paid attention to him. Only a few turned to look at the black smoke rising up the face of the Hotel Azur.

He reached the boulevard and looked toward the

front of the hotel. He hesitated, deciding what to do. To join his uncle and the American or stick to the plan they agreed on. They needed him at the truck. It was their way out of Mosul. But they might need him more inside the hotel. They might be cornered or outgunned, and his rifle would tip the balance.

Or they might be dead.

"You are bleeding, brother." A voice behind him. Arabic.

Hejar turned to see two men close to his age standing behind him. They were clad in black. They had rifles hanging in slings from their shoulders. One wore a web belt, a holster low on his hip like a cowboy gunfighter.

"It is nothing. An old wound. They told me to rest but I did not listen." Hejar spoke Arabic purely, with the thick accent that people told him sounded like a goatherd.

"There is a lot of blood." One of them pointed down the sidewalk. Fresh blots of blood shone black in the dust.

"I will get it bound when I get where I am going." He shifted to move off the curb and cross the boulevard. He fought down a wince. The pain was lancing up to his knee, growing and receding with each beat of his pulse.

"You need stitches, brother."

"A doctor." They moved closer.

"I will be all right. I will be fine. I only need to get back." His hand moved to the pistol grip of his rifle, the palm slimy with sweat from the pain.

"At least let us give you a ride," the gunfighter said.

"Why not?" Hejar said. He hoped his answering smile looked friendly.

51

Levon held a hand up to his friend. He dropped to a knee to pick up bits of white paper that littered the floor of the balcony.

They were trimmed in the shape of flowers, cut by a child's hand.

"This room," he said.

"How can you know?" Bazît said.

"Does it matter?" Levon touched a hand to the handle of the sliding door. The room inside was dark. He gave a gradual tug. The door gave a bit.

He turned to Bazît who nodded, gripped his rifle tighter.

Levon flung the door open and tore the heavy drapes down to the floor. Side-by-side, he and Bazît moved into the dark room. There were two queen beds. The room stank of stale cigarette smoke and staler sweat. Magazines scattered on the floor. A heap of clothing piled in one corner. Bazît kicked the pile. Levon went to a wall and pressed an ear to listen. The gunfire had died to silence as the men searched the floor for them. There was movement in the hallway beyond; men brushed against the wall. Hushed voices in sharp exchanges.

With snapping fingers, Levon got Bazît's attention and pointed him toward the balcony. The Yazidi moved toward the moonlight, rifle raised. Levon flipped one of the mattresses up to place it against the door that connected to the next room. Moving quietly, he braced the second mattress against the door that led to the hallway.

Out on the balcony, Bazît was speaking to someone, calling across the face of the building.

"They are not here. These rooms are empty."

A response Levon could not hear. A high reedy voice trying to sound commanding.

"What is my name? It is Muhammed Ajai. What is yours?"

Another reply.

"I tell you they have left this floor. I will check the stairs."

The voice responded but was moving away back along the balconies the way they had come.

Levon backed against a wall by the door to the bathroom. He reached out to test the knob. Locked. He brought the butt of the M4 down against the knob. The cheap white metal parted at the door surface. The knob dropped to the carpet. He kicked out sending the door crashing inward. With the same motion he ducked low into the dark room, jinking to one side of the frame.

A sink, vanity, commode, and bidet lined one wall. Atop the vanity was a pad of hotel stationery and a pair of scissors. The floor below was littered with bits of paper snipped from the pad.

A stall shower with a surround of frosted glass stood

in the far corner of the room. He approached with his rifle shouldered. In the corner of the shower a dark shape was slumped. He took the phone from his pocket and tabbed it on.

A girl, the girl from the balcony, stared blinking into the blue light. Her eyes were dark under drooping lids; the pupils were black buttons in the center of a tawny corona. Someone had drugged her. The deep stupor formed clouds over her fear.

He lowered his rifle and held out an open hand to her.

"Kani," he said. "Come with me. Your father is here."

———

Hejar sat in the cramped rear seat of a Mercedes. The gunfighter drove with his comrade in the front passenger seat. Music pumped from the speakers front and back. Some kind of rap music. American or French, maybe. Hejar couldn't tell. He gave them directions back to where the truck waited.

"Down here and make a right turn," he said.

"What is the street name?" the gunfighter said.

"I do not know. I have not been here long."

"You cannot remember the street?" the passenger said.

"I cannot read."

The pair in the front seat spoke a rapid exchange in Arabic. Hejar struggled to keep up. He tried to recall the lies that the American made him practice. He was from Yemen to explain his accent and unfamiliarity with Mosul. He came to ISIS with his cousins to fight for

Islam. They sent him out to find batteries for their radio. Hejar sweated as he waited for the questions.

"What do you think of this car, brother?" the gunfighter said, turning his head to offer Hejar a broad grin.

"It is nice. What did you pay for it?"

The pair exploded at that.

"We paid two bullets," the passenger said. He held two fingers up to Hejar. The driver hooted and slapped the steering wheel.

"I would have paid three, but negotiations ended quickly!" They both howled.

"I see. I see." Hejar forced a chuckle at the pair's wit. "Up here. This next street. Make the right turn."

The Mercedes made the turn to creep along a debris-littered alley.

"This is where you stay with your cousins? There are better places, brother," the passenger said.

"Maybe tomorrow we help you find a house nicer than this," the gunfighter said.

"Maybe I will let you get me a good price," Hejar said. "I don't have that many bullets."

They liked that. The gunfighter threw back his head to guffaw. The passenger beat on the dash with his hands.

Hejar reached forward between the seats to pluck the heavy revolver from the driver's holster. He fired twice through the seat backs. The sound in the enclosed place was painfully loud. The passenger was hurled against the dash where his body jerked and seized. The driver's head bounced off the steering wheel and he lay still.

Covering one ear with the palm of his hand, Hejar fired twice more until the passenger lay unmoving across the console between the front seats. He tossed the revolver to the floor. He reached forward to turn the key. The engine and the music died at once.

His leg hurt worse than ever, stiff from just the short time he sat in the car. He clenched his teeth to fight down the urge to whimper as he opened a rear door of the sedan and hobbled away toward the waiting truck.

52

"Where is Rona? Where is your sister?" Bazît shook his daughter by the shoulders.

"She is gone," Kani said. Her voice was just above a murmur. She did not seem to be aware of who was speaking to her.

Levon braced himself against a wall where he could watch the hallway and companion doors. Shuffling of rushing feet and raised voices were louder now. A rattling sound from the hallway. They were testing doors.

"We need to move," he said.

Bazît slapped the girl's face. Once gently. Once not.

"Where has she gone?"

"She did not want to be a bride. She left me."

"Left you? Left you for where?"

The girl was looking past her father, staring at the open window that led to the balcony.

"She's dead," Levon said.

Bazît whirled to him, face ashen.

"She threw herself from the balcony." Levon nodded to the window.

Bazît turned back to his daughter. She was speaking in a monotone.

"They say I am too young to be a bride. My *khus* is not ripe yet. They made me—made me—"

He clamped a hand over her mouth to stop her from saying more. A thin mewling sound rose from deep in his throat. Tears rolled down his clenched face. Blood trickled from where he bit his own lip. His body shook with shame and rage, his eyes locked on his daughter's face with feral intensity.

"Now. We need to leave here," Levon said.

Bazît crushed the little girl to him. He whispered words in her ear too soft for Levon to hear. He broke the hug to speak to Levon in a low voice edged with menace.

"We will go home now."

———

A hand tried the door handle, rattling it up and down. Voices in the hallway rose in volume. Rifle butts battered on the door and frame. They stopped at a shouted command followed by a volley of rapid fire that ripped through the wood around the door lock.

Men crashed through the door and stumbled over the mattress that had been shoved against it. They were in the room in a rush, aiming rifles in all directions. The connecting door to the next room lay open and they charged toward it.

A stream of automatic fire exploded from the open doorway and through the plaster of the shared wall. The compacted crowd of men fell back on one another as those closest to the wall were riddled with multiple rounds. The others were on the floor in a bloody tangle of dying and wounded.

A large man stepped from the other room with a smoking weapon to his shoulder. In a controlled fashion he walked among them pumping rounds into anyone still moving. He stooped to pluck grenades from the lanyards of a vest worn by one of the dead. Three Russian-made frags with a ring pull set inside a bell-shaped plastic cap on a baseball style grenade.

More voices outside the door. He pulled the ring from one of the frags and held it for a one count before sending it in a lob to bounce into the hallway, trailing blue smoke. He dove through the bathroom door; hands clapped over his ears and mouth open wide in a silent shout. A shriek from outside the room was cut short by a bark of thunder that shook the walls and floor.

Levon was up and running through a haze of plaster dust from the ragged holes punched in the walls. He raced through the companion door into the next room. Bazît was there with Kani clutched to him. He kicked down a smoking mattress that he'd thrown up to shield them. Levon led the way to the next companion door and kicked it open. Carrying his daughter, Bazît followed his friend through the next room and into a hallway choked with smoke.

Wailing and cries for help came from the dense fog that filled the hallway with a chemical stink. A hand to the wall, the two men moved away from the voices. A man braced Levon in the smoky dark and asked what had happened. Levon told him that an infidel bomb had struck the hotel and they needed to get a child out to safety. The man blinked through the haze to see Bazît hugging the limp form of Kani to him. He offered to lead the way to a stairwell.

At the stairwell door, the man held the door open for Bazît and his burden to pass. Levon drove the barrel of his Browning into the soft flesh under the man's chin. The Samaritan's brains splashed up the wall and ceiling. Levon was in the stairwell charging down the steps after Bazît and Kani.

They reached the landing of the third floor. Boots rang on the stairs below. Levon pointed right and pushed Bazît and the girl to the exit door. When they were through the doorway, he pulled the pins from his last two grenades and dropped them down the stairwell where they clanged down toward the approaching voices.

A column of smoke rose up, propelled on a confined double blast of concussed air. Broken masonry rained down from above to clatter on the steps and railings.

Through the exit door, Levon hooked right in the dark hallway and caught up with Bazît where two corridors joined. Either the fire at the generator or the grenades discharged in the stairwell had set off the sprinkler system. Water dropped in a fine spray from the ceiling. It only added to the panic, allowing Levon and Bazît to navigate the halls unnoticed.

They found an open stairwell that led down to the second level and a broad mezzanine lobby area. The fuel smoke from the burning generator was thicker here. With the power down, the ventilation system was idle. Visibility dropped to ten feet or less.

A man in a gas mask stepped from the haze. His voice was muffled through the filter vent. Levon tilted his head, a hand to one ear. Speaking with impatience the man stepped within arm's reach. Levon took him by the back of the head and drove the point of a knife into his throat to the hilt. The man trembled once as the spade-shaped blade tore through the flesh and severed his spinal column from his brain.

Lowering the body to the floor, Levon tore the mask from the man's head. He tossed it to Bazît who held it over Kani's face. Her chest rose and fell in shallow breaths. They moved on, blinking back tears that sprang to their eyes in the stinging smoke. They raised their keffiyeh to cover their mouths and noses and trotted away from the source of the densest smoke.

Bazît was in the lead and shouldered open a pair of double doors. Rather than a stairwell, the doors opened onto what was probably a ballroom. It was lit by portable lamps powered by batteries. The high-ceilinged room was lined with rows of tables that served as computer workstations. Laptops, towers, and monitors strung together with yard after yard of bundled cables that ran across the carpeted floor.

And ten believers turned to regard the pair of blood-spattered strangers suddenly appearing in their man cave.

53

Bazît raised his rifle. Levon gripped the end of the barrel and yanked it down, his eyes never leaving the men seated and standing in the room before them.

"Noise discipline," Levon said.

Bazît tore his weapon from Levon's hand with a growl. He seethed through clenched teeth. He held it on the startled men, his finger resting outside the trigger guard.

"Step away! Against the wall! This way!" Levon barked commands, gesturing with his rifle.

There were no firearms in sight. This room was a techno-lair. Dead now, the keyboards and monitors were their weapons of mass destruction. From here they struck out at their enemies, the great Satans, by spreading lies and recruiting new fighters.

The men moved from their stations toward the wall. Some eyed the intruders with open loathing. Most of them were round-eyed in fear, their eyes on the strangers' weapons.

"Backs against the wall! On your knees! Now!"

They did as they were told. Bazît kept his weapon trained on them, his daughter mute by his side. Levon worked down the line, making them drop to their knees.

"Hands behind your backs!" One of them made a move to stand. Levon stroked him across the forehead with a rifle butt. The man collapsed with a hollow groan. A second downward slam to the back of the neck silenced him. Every man did as he was ordered, knees on the ground and hands clasped behind them.

Levon told Bazît to make sure the door they entered was secure. The Yazidi made for the doorway, Kani keeping close behind him. Bazît shot the bolts on the doors and piled a few chairs against them.

"Lift your heads. Look at me." Levon moved down the row of men, capturing images of them on the phone. They offered baleful looks before wincing as the flash popped inches from their faces. One of them wore a reflexive smile for his portrait out of habit.

"What are we doing? Why do we not kill them and leave?" Bazît said in whispered Kurd.

"You want them all dead? This is how we will make that happen," Levon said.

"I can shoot them. Right now."

"I mean every one of them. Every Daesh in this building." Levon cradled his rifle to leave his hands free to key tabs on the phone's screen.

"How is that possible? There are maybe hundreds."

"Ever hear of 'broken arrow'?" Levon said the last in English.

"What is that in my language?"

"Not sure. Think of something very bad."

"*Cehnem*. That is our word for where demons live."

"That about covers it. I'm almost done here."

Levon held the phone up to take a photo of himself then set the phone onto the corner of a table. Together, he and Bazît emptied their rifles into the row of kneeling men. Kani flinched at the long bursts of fire, watching the men as they died. Her eyes were as dead as a doll's, as if she were blind to anyone's pain but her own. Before her father could snatch her up into his arms, she rushed forward to kick at one of the fallen men. Bazît carried her from the room over his shoulder. She spat back at the row of corpses sagged against the wall.

There were gas masks still in plastic wrappers at some of the workstations. Levon grabbed a mask for himself and tossed another to Bazît. They exited the ballroom into a corridor that ran behind the back of the room toward the hotel's kitchens. Smoke was thick along the ceiling. They took a moment to fix Kani's mask in place and then their own.

"Where do we go now?" Bazît said.

"As far from here as possible. The demons are about to come home," Levon said.

———

It was good to be king.

Or at least one of eight deputy directors at the NSA. One of the perks was a primo slot in the executive parking area a short walk from the employee exit. He was grateful that his three-year-old Subaru wasn't a hike away in the peon lots that spread out across the Maryland hills.

Brett Tsukuda had his tie off, car keys in hand, and was ready to call it a day. It was just after seven in the evening and the end of a sixteen-hour day of briefings, meetings, intelligence reviews and threat analysis. He'd actually get home before the kids went to bed tonight.

"Sir! Sir!"

He turned to the uniformed guard jingling toward him across the dark lot from the building.

"Shit," Brett said.

The guard escorted Brett up to the secure situation room on the third floor and saw him inside, the vault type door closing behind him. It was going to be a long night. He was already regretting skipping lunch. The men around the table didn't give him any hope that he'd see home anytime tonight. Two other deputy directors and the director himself. A phone was jacked into a speaker crouching in the center of the table on spider legs. Not *a* phone. *The* phone.

"I'm told you can verify this, Brett," the director said. He turned to a monitor on the wall and tabbed a remote.

A cell phone video in portrait mode began. Dim colors flashed across the scene before the phone came to rest on the face of a kneeling man. He squinted as a flash exploded inches from his face. This sequence repeated ten times as the video played out. The image paused on a man captured in the flash of light. The last man was lying on a carpeted floor, unconscious with blood on his face.

"What am I looking at?" Brett said.

"This video was time-stamped less than twenty minutes ago. GPS tells us it was taken in Mosul," the director said.

"This is in your wheelhouse, Brett. Do you know any of these faces? Any ISIL players you know? said a left-over deputy director who insisted on referring to the

Islamic State by the acronym preferred by the previous administration.

"What's facial recognition say?" Brett said.

"Still waiting on that. Can you pick anyone out?" the director said.

"Take the video back to number four. No, further back. Number three. Yeah. Him."

The image froze on the face of a man with a dark beard streaked with gray. His expression of pure bile was more malignant than the others.

"That's Abd al Bari Sarraf," Brett said. "Yemeni national. A half-ass, self-appointed emir. Evidence points to him as the main actor in some of the beheadings they put on the net. We have him located in Mosul at last reports."

"What about the other faces?" the director said.

"I recognize a few others here. Some are new to me. But if they're hanging with Bari Sarraf, they're *all* bad news."

"He's a priority target then," the voice on the speakerphone said.

"He is, sir," Brett said to the speaker.

"Then I'm greenlighting this. Right now," the president of the United States said from the speaker.

"But what confirmation do we have on this? I mean, where did this video *come* from?" Brett said.

"It showed up in your inbox. No message. Just the video attached," the director said.

"Do it. Final word." The speakerphone went dead with a click.

"*My* inbox? Who in Mosul has *my* email?" Brett said.

"We were hoping you could tell us that," the director said. He turned back to the screen and tabbed the remote. The video advanced until the image of a grim-faced man appeared in the frame. The man on the screen said nothing. He only regarded the men in the room with hard eyes. Then the screen went dark before lighting up again with a wallpaper image of the sun setting over the ocean between palm trees.

"Holy shit." Brett sank into a chair.

"So, you do know this guy?" the director said.

"Oh yeah."

"How?" the leftover said.

"No time for that," the director said. "Your call, Brett. Does *his* presence on the ground confirm that this is an actionable mission probability?"

"Like the word of God on high," Brett said.

The director touched a keypad by his hand.

"Get me Quantico and Navy Intel now," the director said.

54

The Tomahawk launched off the deck of the destroyer created a false dawn seen from the mainland. For miles around the ship, the Med turned from midnight to high noon. The star-bright object rose high toward space on a hyper-sonic course before dropping in a controlled descent toward its target.

———

Yasin and Zamir stood in the crowd of men watching the hotel burn. Yasin clasped his little brother's hand tightly in his so they would not become separated in the crowd jostling to bear witness. It was well past curfew, but the boys risked punishment to watch the blaze high above.

The upper floors were fully consumed by flames. A tower of black smoke blotted out the stars. Ash and embers fluttered down onto the street and rooftops. Explosions within the building could be felt as well as heard. Showers of sparks bloomed from windows sending broken shards to drop down in a crystalline rain of tinkling glass.

Men streamed out of the hotel through a thick haze of smoke, faces covered with their shirt fronts. Other men came from the crowd with bottles of water to help them wash ash from their eyes and mouths. Despite the danger, there was a festive atmosphere for the men watching the fire. No effort was made to save the building. ISIS was many things but serving as volunteer firemen was not among their missions.

Some shook fists and made dire threats of God's wrath upon the infidels who caused the fire. But most were enjoying the spectacle and shared experience. They oohed and pointed as though watching a fireworks display. Some fired their rifles into the air, caught up in the moment. The French hotel was, after everything else, a symbol of the kind of colonial oppression they had been taught to hate. And hate trumped everything else. They longed for, thirsted for, objects for their rage. A burning infidel hotel was red meat for them.

Yasin watched a pair of men rush from the smoke. They wore gas masks that gave them a comical look like cartoon ducks. One of the men carried a young girl in his arms, her face strapped with a mask as well. They ran across the boulevard from the hotel. The larger of the men turned his goggle eyes toward Yasin. He parted from the other man and ran to where the two boys stood. The other man, carrying the girl, waded deep into the men crowded in the street.

The big man stepped directly to Yasin and caught his arm in an iron grip. Yasin tried to pull away, his own hold on his little brother's arm tightened.

The man lifted his mask. It was the man, the white man, from the rooftop.

"Run," the man said. He released Yasin's arm and wedged himself into the crowd and was gone.

Yasin yanked his brother's arm and together they ran. They ran hard and they ran far.

They were blocks away when they were knocked flat to the pavement by a shockwave that roiled the ground like an ocean wave. Windows all along both sides of the street shattered in an all-encompassing din louder than thunder. Yasin raised himself from the ground on skinned knees. His brother was crying, holding hands clapped over his ears.

His brother's crying was silent. The world was silent. The only sound was a high-pitched whine wavering in his ears.

He looked back toward the burning hotel. All that remained was a cloud of gray dust rising from the ground. The fire was gone now. The building was gone.

55

Gunny Leffertz said:

"Ain't no better feeling than being alive after so many wished you evil."

"You look like shit," Hector Ortiz said.

"Don't you have a job somewhere?" Levon said.

"It can wait."

"How'd you find me?"

"I heard some crazy gringo motherfucker came into camp with a little girl."

Hector found Levon outside an aid station near the Yazidi encampment. Levon was still in his filthy clothes, his hair matted with other men's blood. He took water and a plate of food from the volunteers but wouldn't move from his place outside the tents.

"Your friend only found one of his daughters?" Hector said.

"The other one committed suicide weeks ago."

"Shit. That's a tough one."

"Bazît's in there with her. She's dehydrated and detoxing. They kept her drugged. I'm hoping that means she doesn't remember much."

"Fuck," Hector said.

A tent flap parted. Hejar hobbled to Levon, an aluminum crutch under his arm, his leg stiff with a cast from knee to ankle. The back of his hand was bleeding from where he'd torn an IV line out.

"He wants to see you," Hejar said.

Levon left Hector to follow the boy to the tent.

———

The girl looked younger than she had back at the Azur. Younger and more fragile. Color back in her skin. The black clothing was gone. Her thin arms and legs were bare under a simple white shift. Purple bruises with a yellow halo on her wrists. She had been bathed and her hair washed and combed. A hydration line had been run into her arm.

"She will be fine. Her body anyway," Bazît said. His eyes did not leave his daughter as he spoke.

"What will you do? Will you go back to your work?" Levon said.

"This is not the end. Oh, Daesh will leave Mosul and Sinjar this year or next. But there is much more to do."

"What about Kani?"

"I have family in Kirkuk. I will take her there, stay with her until she is well."

"And you?"

"The Kurds have risen, taken their place in the fight

against the Sunni. The Yazidis have as well. This is the beginning of the fight, not the end. The Arab will come for us. The Turk too. I will carry a rifle."

Levon said nothing. Bazît turned from the sleeping girl on the cot to look at Levon.

"There are no words for what you have done for me, Levon Cade. I could spend a lifetime and not express my gratitude in full."

"Not about getting even. I was only making good on my word. That's all."

Bazît gripped his friend by the arm.

"You must make me a new promise."

Levon looked into his friend's red-rimmed eyes.

"You must promise me, Levon Cade, that you will never return to Iraq."

Levon nodded.

56

Nancy Valdez sat in her cubicle, sipping tepid coffee. Her desktop was clean. The computer tower, keyboard, and monitor gone. A sad little box of her personal possessions sat on the floor by her chair. A double row of cardboard file boxes lined one wall. All neatly taped and labeled with case number and dates. Her final job as task force leader was to wait until some marshals came to haul the boxes away.

Laura leaned into the entrance to her cubicle.

"We're going to dinner when this over," Laura said.

"Marcoon too?"

"Yeah."

"So, you're going to get drunk."

"Maybe. Yeah. You coming with?"

"No, thanks," Nancy said.

"Do you good."

"Trust me, you do not want *my* company tonight."

"Did they reassign you?" Laura took a seat in the guest chair.

"A counterfeit case in Des Moines. It'll get me out of DC awhile."

"Not me or Chad. It's back to staring into a monitor eight hours a day for us. Tony's talking about early retirement."

"Sorry. Sorry to all of you."

"It was worth it, Nancy. I'll miss it but it was a trip while it lasted. We were like real detectives."

"But we didn't get to solve the mystery."

"Yeah. I'm going to have a hard time sleeping for a while over that." Laura stood now.

"We all are. Well, maybe not Chad."

"You sure you're good?" Laura paused at the cubicle opening.

"Go, go!" Nancy said. She fixed a smile on her face, made shoo-shoo motions with her hands. And Laura was gone.

She was left alone with her thoughts. A case without a resolution. A mystery with no more clues. She hated that. Most of all, she hated the bureaucracy that prevented her from staying on the case. Hated them for pulling her back when she was so close. And more than that, the painful realization that she would never know *why* her team was pulled off of Levon Cade so abruptly.

They'd shit-canned her investigation at a meeting first thing that morning. She was called into unit supervisor Sylvester's office, but he wasn't there. Instead, a deputy director himself gave her the bad news. There were two men with him that she was not introduced to. They wore visitor badges. The deputy director did not defer to them directly, but the vibe was there. They were in charge.

"We're going to handle this through other channels," the deputy director said.

"Another section in Treasury, sir?"

"That's need-to-know. You've done solid work here, but it's been decided that this will move forward elsewhere."

"Will the new investigation take over the tap on George Cade?"

"Who is that?"

"The uncle, sir. The suspect's last known address."

"No. We're off that tap." He glanced at the two visitors. One of them nodded. One nod.

"Yes, sir," Nancy said.

"Thank you, Agent Valdez. Trust me that your work on this will be remembered."

Back at her desk, she ran that meeting over in her mind. Someone pulled the plug on her; someone way up the chain. She'd probably never know who or why. She'd have to find peace with that. But that peace was a long way off. It wasn't something she'd find in Iowa chasing funny money.

A pair of uniformed officers came with a hand truck for her file cartons. She took up her box of personal items and made her way downstairs and out through the security exit. It was drizzling on the street as she made her way to the parking garage on H Street. The box went into the trunk of her car. It would come out when they assigned her a new desk once she was back from Iowa. If she ever came back from Iowa.

The drizzle built to a drumming downpour that hammered down on her car as she drove out onto the street. She sat in the beep and creep traffic watching the rain streak the grime on her windshield. She dug in her coat for her phone, tabbed the screen on. Her thumb scrolled down to Bill Marquez's number and hovered there for a breath or two.

"Shit."

She tossed the phone onto the dash and pulled through the intersection toward the Beltway and home.

Merry stepped into the stall, her nose wrinkled in deep disapproval.

"Uncle Fern let Montana get fat," she said.

"She's healthy otherwise. You'll ride that off in a few weeks," Jessie said. She handed Merry a bridle over the stall wall.

Merry bridled the pony while Jessie threw a blanket over the animal's back. Together they cinched the saddle in place and Merry led the pony out into the crisp afternoon. Junebug, the spotted Alpine goat, skipped to the edge of the wire fence and bleated after them. They walked to a waiting trailer, the back door open and ramp down.

"The long trail still has snow on it," Jessie said.

"Short trail's fine. Sandy coming with us?"

"She said she is. I hope she is. She promised to get Brewster and that new roan ready to ride."

They were coaxing the pony, its ears plastered back, up onto the ramp with kind words and a handful of hay when Uncle Fern called from the porch of the cabin.

"Phone call for you, Merry!"

He held the door for her, a smile wrinkling his face. She ran past him to snatch up the kitchen phone. Merry listened for a bit, the phone clutched tight to her ear. Her eyes got wider as she listened.

"Daddy!"

ABOUT THE AUTHOR

Born and raised in Philadelphia, Chuck Dixon worked a variety of jobs from driving an ice cream truck to working graveyard at a 7-11 before trying his hand as a writer. After a brief sojourn in children's books he turned to his childhood love of comic books. In his thirty years as a writer for Marvel, DC Comics and other publishers, Chuck built a reputation as a prolific and versatile freelancer working on a wide variety titles and genres from Conan the Barbarian to SpongeBob Square-Pants. His graphic novel adaptation of J.R.R. Tolkien's *The Hobbit* continues to be an international bestseller translated into fifty languages. He is the co-creator (with Graham Nolan) of the Batman villain Bane, the first enduring member added to the Dark Knight's rogue's gallery in forty years. He was also one of the seminal writers responsible for the continuing popularity of Marvel Comics' The Punisher.

After making his name in comics, Chuck moved to prose in 2011 and has since written over twenty novels, mostly in the action-thriller genre with a few side-trips to horror, hardboiled noir and western. The transition from the comics form to prose has been a life-altering event for him. As Chuck says, *"writing a comic is like getting on a roller coaster while writing a novel is more like a long car trip with a bunch of people you'll learn to hate."* His

Levon Cade novels are currently in production as a television series from Sylvester Stallone's Balboa Productions. He currently lives in central Florida and, no, he does not miss the snow.

Printed in Great Britain
by Amazon

49693829R00160